Bend This Heart

SHORT STORIES BY JONIS AGEE

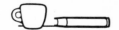

Coffee House Press :: Minneapolis :: 1989

The publisher thanks the following organizations whose support helped make this book possible: The National Endowment
for the Arts, a federal agency; The Jerome Foundation; and
United Arts.

The author thanks Brenda, Jackie, Cindy, Paul, Lon and Susan
for their support, understanding and advice.

Coffee House Press books are distributed to trade by Consortium
Book Sales and Distribution, 213 East Fourth Street, Saint Paul,
Minnesota 55101. Our books are also available through all major
library distributors and jobbers, and through most small press
distributors, including Bookpeople, Bookslinger, Inland, Pacific
Pipeline, and Small Press Distribution. For personal orders, cat-
alogs or other information, write to Coffee House Press, 27 North
Fourth Street, Suite 400, Minneapolis, Mn 55458.

Library of Congress Cataloging in Publication Data

Agee, Jonis
    Bend this heart : short stories / by Jonis Agee.
        p. cm.
    ISBN 0-918273-51-X : $9.95
    1. Love stories, American. I. Title.
PS3551.G4B46   1989
813'.54 – dc20   89-7100
                        CIP

Short Story Index
1989-1993

Contents

For Celia

I Can't Stop Loving You

FOR TWO YEARS I lived in a neighborhood of lovers. You could tell love was everywhere. Matching sixties Cadillac convertibles arrived and mated every spring beside the tiny corner house. Each one claimed by a short fat member of the husband-wife team who built the swimming pool, which consumed the backyard, and the stockade fence, which hid their cooing and the tanning of sausage-round limbs. Only the ballpark-size floodlight was shared, like a full moon on dark nights.

In my house we were having none of that. I had retired from love, from friends. I was busy eating, being alone with the television's sympathetic light bathing me blue and more as I slept on the sofa. Once I left the door unlocked, and as if it spread its arms to the sidewalk like a net, it caught a man, whose clumping steps announced him. A mistake. Even the six-pack under his arm. "It's not my fault," he declared. "You should keep your door locked." I agreed as I let him out, hoping he'd find the woman he was after.

Next door, Patrick kept the gardens just the way she had, although he gave all the vegetables away and spent weekends with a former wife. There was her memory to be serviced like a lawn being kept neat. After a while he shoveled my snow too, even advancing to sweep the porch when I wasn't around. I bought chocolate chips and made cookies for him, over and over, eating them every time in a fit of shyness. Now I can't remember delivering a single plate to his door, though I might have taken one—the scene is so clear the way I knew it would be.

Across the street real love took place. Cyndie made men swoon from her second-story balcony. Left the lights on all night long, came home when it pleased her. Sunbathed all summer day and drove off at dusk in her little red sports car. When we woke up at dawn, there was always a strange car parked for her—electricians, carpenters, salesmen, a few times even a chauffeur whose long black limo crowded our tiny curbs and old cars like a bully newly moved in. Cyndie's soft Czech limbs and wild honey hair wound the male dreams of our neighborhood onto a tight spool and saved them from the temptations of the massage parlor three blocks away.

One night when storm sirens brought us all to our front porches, I saw Cyndie's lover wheel his motorcycle into the shelter of the garage, his black leather pants bleeding dark into the shadows of the house as his white back and shaved skull blinked, "Touch me, take me." Later they grilled steaks under the shelter of her second-story porch and left the light on all night long. Inside my house I watched storm warnings roll like credits along the bottom of the television screen.

Directly across from me lived one of the true lovers of this story. His love streamed out of his garage, on forties music: an aging Frank Sinatra with a drink-ballooned body, tousled black hair—it was never quite the day he'd washed it—and desire he wore like a tattoo for everyone to see. I met him at the corner store in my riding boots. He never forgot. It became a bond between us, a secret—what I knew he knew. At night I undressed in the windows facing his, with the lights on. Summers the trees might screen me, winters, the frost.

We never spoke directly, except for the times late at night he called me. I was alone. I should have been asleep. I had left the lights on, the door locked. That stopped when he got a girlfriend.

How do we know?

It was his violence of loving. When they fought, he threw her clothes into the alley and lit them on fire, emptied the contents of the house and his heart on the tiny lawn at three o'clock in the morning, then rode his bicycle like a drunken acrobat up and down the alleys until dawn. Once I almost hit him. And like our neighbors it was the gift of locomotion that betrayed him: the beat-up Datsun he bestowed on the woman's daughter. It lurked like a bird by the curb in repair, rusted, unhinged, pounded with luck and love. It received his attention almost daily.

Down the block, Huey and his mother waged the wars of love too, in a house dislocated from time, the Fourth of July flag leaning crazily against the plastic jack-o'-lantern on the front porch all year long. Inside, there were paths like jungle trails through the shoulder-high newspapers. Huey sold drugs, and his mother gathered the neighborhood gossip, until her body went bad and she had to be carried around like a bag-lady version of Cleopatra on the arms of Huey and his freaked-out motorcycle friends. When the bars closed, Huey opened his doors. Later he cursed his love to the moon and stars, cursed the Vietnamese, the United States government and someone trying to OD in his front yard. It did no good to call the police. They'd known Huey all their lives. "He's crazy. He's always been crazy." They drove awar. On Sundays, Huey and his mother fought all day long.

Finally she firebombed his motorcycle, parked under a tree out front. The stain of black remained on the leaves and bark until winter. Huey stayed put, though, his transportation gone. He used his mother's car. Driving her on her daily rounds, he was clearly in love, as he peered crazily ahead and didn't quite brake for the stop signs that patrolled our tiny block at either end.

An apprentice at love in that neighborhood, I went on a diet. I talked to no one I used to know. When my car was wrecked, I figured it was a good sign, an act of love, a promise of more to come. And when I met someone finally, I trapped his heart like a small animal and held it, held it, held it.

And Blue

DOWNSTAIRS Reba's ex-husband is watching soap operas.
He's been at it for two hours. Doesn't bother to apologize
when she walks in the door. His favorite is *One Life to Live.*
He's a Buddhist. Going to be a monk, he says, when he's too
old for sex. Some of the far-out ones still screw around, he
adds. It's no use trying to figure out if he means himself,
Reba decides and walks through the neat piles of bedding
and clothes he sandbags along the walls and bookcases as if
there's going to be a flood. She doesn't like it about herself
that she finds his things a little nasty.

Reba is lying in bed watching blue cabbages of light bom-
bard the dark field that appears when she closes her eyes.
Maybe they're asteroids. She hears creaking in the hallway
but ignores it. She'll find out soon enough.

"I'm coming through there on my way east," he'd said.
"I'm going into real estate, going to sell."

"Get a haircut," she'd advised. Reba wonders if buddhists
sell only to each other. A secret network or something.

Her new husband doesn't mind the ex on the sofa. Does
this mean the romance is over? she wonders.

Twenty-five years ago, when she was pregnant, Reba
would stay up all night, go to sleep at dawn, wake up just
when the heat began to close its hand around the apartment.

She'd eat Jell-O and turn on the television for the afternoon soaps. Every day the same thing. It hurt her when the weekend came and the day stretched like a yawn she couldn't close her mouth against. Her ex was a Baptist then. When he voted for Barry Goldwater and lost, she felt triumph and pity. He didn't know what was good for him.

Upstairs Reba thinks everyone is tucked in an envelope, waiting for the tongue that licks the edges and seals the letter. Her daughter watches soaps in her room, but they're different ones, so she can't watch with her father in the living room. She likes *The Young and the Restless.* They all have good hairdos on that one.

"I hope she finds out where she's going," Reba's ex says. "I'm forty-five, and I still don't know."

As Reba drives him to the grocery store, he asks, "Do you ever think about the void, nothingness?"

She concentrates on her driving—stop at the light, move over one lane to avoid the turning truck, pull around on the green, swing back into the lane, and turn into the parking lot.

"No," she says, "I'm too busy."

He's careful just to eat leftovers. Won't start a meal of fresh food on his own. "Where's the asparagus from last night?" he asks her three times one morning. There's panic in his voice.

"Make yourself some bacon and eggs," she tells him.

"Is it okay if I eat that leftover hamburger?" he asks.

Reba catches her name on a page he is writing in his cramped, childish handwriting, as though a right-handed person was forced to do it left, though he *is* left-handed. She feels him disapproving of her.

"Can we have vegetables tonight?" he asks.

"We had them last night. Artichokes, remember?"

He nods, unconvinced, then goes back to writing. Later she catches her new husband's name on the page too. He thinks they spend too much money. She knows he's read the bills, her mail. She doesn't know how to tell him it's okay.

When the painters come one day, her ex is full of advice. He sneaks inspections and pulls her from her work to discipline the men in the basement for not doing the job the way they should.

"There's no reason why they can't do it right," he says. He is sitting on the living-room floor combing out the gray rug fuzz packed in the vacuum-cleaner attachment. She notices that he's using his own little black pocket comb. He does this for an hour. "I bet no one's ever done this, have they?" he says.

"No, but it hasn't hurt it. Ten years and it still works fine. What difference does it make?"

"It makes a difference," he assures her. "Ten years, huh?"

"We've never done it," she tells him. "Why don't you just vacuum?" The pile of fuzz grows slowly beside him. It is so small she would have missed it on the mottled tan rug if it weren't outlined against his leg.

An hour later when he vacuums, he does such a poor job Reba can hardly tell it's been done.

At noon when she comes back from work, she asks him if he's eaten. "Ice cream, brownies, cake," he tells her. Leftovers.

When Reba can't sleep at dawn, sneaking downstairs to grab a cup of tea, he is awake, dressed. This happens every morning, although the hour varies wildly. His bed is neatly folded, and he is sitting cross-legged in the living room, facing the floor-to-ceiling draw drapes in the gloom. She wonders if this is a trick he is learning. Or if he's like a household dog, always awake a minute before the master.

On Saturday night they order Vietnamese food. The ex doesn't know any of the dishes on the take-out menu and asks for their help. He eats judiciously, saving the stuff at the bottom of his cartons for the next day.

In three days her ex does not use the towel or the wash-cloth Reba's set out for him. She notices that he doesn't smell. She worries that maybe he is using her towel. She tests it for dampness each time she goes to the bathroom, hesitating a moment before she holds the towel up to her face. She doesn't want the odor of him in her mouth—the gray metal slice of sweat souring like wet diapers with Dial soap rubbed dry over it. Even now as she tests the towel, she is afraid of it pressing its big body against her face. She waits for him to take a bath and leave the room steamy and sour for hours after.

There was only one year when Reba liked his smell. They would bathe together, him in front, her in back, the reverse of her husband now. She would groom the blackheads from his back, washing each red pinched spot carefully with soap and hot water. In this way she cleared up the last of his adolescent skin troubles.

The smell hadn't appeared really until their divorce, when he spent three months in a windowless room in the base-ment of a house, after she'd kicked him out. First he shaved his head, then put on his wool sweaters, although it was late spring and hot. Then madness appeared in his eyes and on his skin. He chased her on his bike all over town, in and out of the beds of other men, until they were both exhausted and she let him back in the house for the summer. It was then that Reba noticed he wore the smell like a permanent stain on his clothes or like a birthmark, glass of wine spilled across his skin.

For twenty years he has been coming to visit Reba this way. She is beginning to feel sorry for him. The way his hair and beard hang ragged around his worn collar. The way he neatly folds his wide workman's leather belt. The way his work boots have begun to split and crack along the sole lines. The way he hunches over, his hands clenched as he watches the progress of the couples on his favorite soap.

Stop Loving Me

THE SUN comes up on some wet corner of the universe, and I'm supposed to rejoice. "Tell the little bastards to keep their their hands to themselves." That's what I should've said. Sure, there's traffic everywhere. I count the cars when I got nothing else to do.

One morning I'm lying there on the sofa, you know, like I do when he leaves, so he don't know it's me making all the dirt, and I think, Oh, it comes in waves, according to what shift the dumb wankers are due in. Suits. Elephants. I know what they call them. I did plenty of it in my time. Now I lie on the sofa and listen to the cars coming and going like water on the Jersey shore.

Sure, he said we'd go there sometime. "Before I die," I wanted to tell him. "*Before* that."

Then I go in and make myself a cup of tea. I don't call it a "nice" cup of tea, because it sure is going to upset the stomach. Besides, I ain't no old lady – not in this mood I'm not. So it's not a nice cup. I take out the spoon with the snap head like a duck's bill. Once I went after him with it, *quack-quacking*. He got this look. You've never seen such a look as he got then. I stopped, put it away. I just put the loose tea in it, anyway. It's nothing.

We got this fussy old tree out front. Really. You can tell how it is just by the dangle of the limbs some days. Fussy thing. Drops these little twigs all over and won't let a blade of grass through. Shades everything. Thinks it's God though, like some fancy old lady—a pinch of twig here, a pinch there. Fussy. When it didn't rain all last summer, he said, "Water the tree."

I wanted to say, "Water it yourself. It's so damn particular, let it wilt."

I go to the doctor. He says, "What're you fighting now? You and him at it?"

"No, nothing's going on. I just don't feel good." Can't I say that?

He looks out the little window that's fixed up with a wooden shutter like it's in someone's house out in the suburbs and not this old tacky block building in the middle of town. Then he writes something down in this folder. I try to read it upside down, but it don't work. Code. I figure it's a code. Especially when he glances my way, as I'm rummaging through my purse. He thinks I don't notice him looking. "Listen, I know about the car waves," I want to tell him.

You can't put anything over on me. At the store they try. I make them get the manager. He says it real carefully: "The sign means that the hams are five pounds, not that they're on sale for five dollars. The hams are seven dollars like they're marked there on the can." I watched the cashier girl pull him down the aisle by the sleeve. He didn't want to come. I don't blame him. I pull out a twenty to pay the extra two dollars. The people behind me shift their weight and sigh. They're tired of it. "Well so am I," I want to tell them. "So am I."

As I look around while she's packing up the groceries for me, one woman smiles at me. Sure. Why not? I smile back. We understand each other. Nothing needs to be said. I pull the collar of my camel-hair up and push the cart of groceries out ahead of me like it's a little kid that needs steering, because I sure intend to walk it too fast. That's the way I am.

"You always look so nice," they tell me.

"Ha, you should see me at home," I want to say. I let myself go. Slouch around with my hair on end like one of the Three Stooges—I forget which. I go into the bathroom every once in a while just to check. Sure enough, I'm as awful as before. Nothing's fallen into place. I like that. I scratch myself and let my face get old. It does, you know— falls down on its knees and sits there in a puddle. I let my stomach go too, stick it out, proud, and make myself feel greasy and hopeless. I lie on the couch and listen to folks going crazy to work. Listen to that fussy tree bang against the house like a dog trying to get back in the door. Listen to the boiler send the heat rushing up. Steam like a snake goes writhing through the house, rubbing all the windows shut with moisture.

I let it get too hot, almost too much to breathe. I can feel it trying to crawl in like lint and line my lungs. Then I get up and turn it off. Make it go back in its hole. The window shades are hanging real limp then. Reminds you of a flag on the Fourth of July. Too hot, not a breath of air. There's no parade, though. Nothing's going to come marching through here but me. And I won't give the satisfaction.

In The Blood

WHEN HE HAD first gotten back, they felt new and strange to each other. It wasn't just that each was five years older, more worn and more certain about life now than in their earlier years. No, it was also the fact of where he had been and how far she had gone on, living in their house and raising their children alone, although for him she was still there as five years before. Somehow he was confident that the threads of feeling remained unbroken and attached as ever between them.

He imagined her body clean lined, though it had never been, and smooth, though she had always had scars and rough, bumpy patches of skin. She was uncomfortable and flattered.

When they made love, she imagined him entering the soft fine bodies of the women he must have known. She imagined him coming at them slowly, his dirty hands and face smudging their cleanness and mingling with their perfume. When he took off his clothes, she tried not to look at the fresh purple scars etched like insect trails along his legs. There had been a wound. A deep and hollow scar, white and strange, stood on one shoulder blade, and if she were not careful, her hand would slip into its cup as she smoothed the muscles on his back. Now she closed her eyes always when they made love. She could not stand the love eating into her like a dog not fed for too many days—this dog living in his eyes, becoming his eyes, the pitiable and the alien, some thirsty and hungry creature intent on feeding itself more than anything else, like the dog she had once accidentally locked in the garage for a weekend when she had gone away, the forgiveness and the starvation together she saw in its face on Monday morning. It had probably stopped howling after a day, when its throat had burned out. She could see the claw marks on the doors and the chewed edges of wood. His teeth had caught and torn the loose skin surrounding his gums. The blood, dried by then, matted the white hairs on his chin. In his frenzy he must have torn out several nails, because his paws were bloody too. And in his anguish of abandonment he had progressed to the diarrhea standing in pools on the concrete floor of the garage, when he must have been certain of his own death. But she had come back, had found him, and had taken him into the house for his food and water, and as he ate, she saw that look—too hungry for what she had offered it.

She felt him feeding on her breasts, biting softly and sucking, trying to drain her into his mouth, and she knew it was not enough. Even when he grew violent, while she lay on her stomach and he hammered himself into her buttocks, she knew that he was growing more afraid of the love he wanted. The only act he really allowed her was to let her use her mouth on him, and after he had emptied himself into her in that way, helpless to her comfort and succored by her tongue, releasing himself into the fear of her teeth, then he could be full. Sometimes he told her afterward that it was like walking down a forest trail, knowing that assassins were waiting for him, yet he could not keep from walking down the trail, smelling the urgent growth of vegetation, seeing the flowers and butterflies, and hearing the birds whose hasty cries could be the end.

She performed this act for him nightly after a while, and somehow it soothed him into his sleep. He could endure the days that way. His life became possible. Like the dog she had recovered from the garage, he became obedient and gentle. But always a little hunger lingered about his mouth, rested in his eyes.

It was two years later that they found out about the thing in his blood. They had gone on with their life, more than less comfortable, accepting the things that had happened, more or less. She sometimes felt tired at night and went to sleep immediately instead of making love with him. These nights he lay awake for hours, but he was beginning to forget the past. What he had lived through had become almost a familiar and comfortable fantasy on those nights of thinking. Often he found that just recalling it would give him an erection, which he would have to somehow dissolve before sleep. A couple of times he watched her sleeping, sometimes frowning, with her mouth slightly open and vulnerable to him at any moment he might choose. The slight pressing of a nipple against her nylon gown as she breathed in and out he would watch for a long time, the rhythm of its coming and going, until he ejaculated. And sometimes, when it was warm and she was in a deep sleep, her eyes fluttering behind the lids in dreaming, he would carefully draw back the covers and hold his penis over her breast or mouth.

Although the cancer in his blood required care from his physician, it didn't stop him from working, only made him tired and sometimes sick. But it also made him more sexual than ever. Now he wanted her all the time. As he lost weight, as he ate less, he grew more frantic about her love and her body. On the other hand, after the disease was discovered, she began to be afraid, even revulsed by the one act which could appease him. As if she now had to feed the dog from her own mouth, eat his fear, she could not bear on her tongue the liquid sex, filled, she imagined, with his blood and webbed with his sickness. She thought of how she had grown afraid of the dog, which, no matter how much she fed it, did not regain its weight. She eventually left the dog in the small wire cage at the Humane Society, panting from its starvation. Now her husband was like a dog let out of a cage, tracking her down, but as if her stomach were always full and bursting, she could not bear to open her mouth to him, and her body ached as if it had been filled with stones.

Hunting Story

THE SUNLIGHT lay in white tiles across the snowy fields in front of him. Bronk squinted once more and squeezed the trigger. "There. And one for the little girl who lived in the lane," he whispered, as the buckshot fluffed the feathers of the goose, *poof*, like a pillow his mother plumped and settled on the bed. The goose collapsed, its head going down in slow motion, like a giraffe descending. Then it simply stopped in the water and floated.

For a moment the other geese didn't move. Then the sound wave caught up. They flapped and rose in a single breath, as if carried on one wing rather than twenty. He shot over and over, squeezing the trigger with an abandon he'd never known. One for his mother, the naked whiteness in its bath, the long legs that never lost their shape. One for the lady, then. And goose after goose plumped, *poofed*, staggered in midair and dropped from its rising arc.

And the last one, Bronk thought, as instinct told him he was out of shells, no more pumping of the two guns. He squeezed the last one. And this for the sister, the one who waited, one for the dame, one for the master, one for the little girl who lived down the . . . He watched it falter, flapping too hard for a moment in disappointment at falling behind the others, the few who had escaped his harvest. It *squacked* once, twice, then froze and fell clumsily, tumbling in an awkward spin of wings and neck. When it hit the water, it sank, unlike the others which still floated among the decoys and weeds. But damn. Thing sank. Wasn't supposed to do that.

"Go get 'em now." He gestured to the pond, and his uncle Bill's black Lab jumped up from the blind and leaped into the freezing water. Swimming with its head held furiously out of the water, the dog paddled to the covey of dead birds, picked the first one delicately with its teeth, lips held in a grimace away from the feathers, turned and headed back for the blind. It was going to take a while this way. If he'd only brought both dogs—but he hadn't wanted to invite his uncle, his father's stepbrother. Like an older brother, his Uncle Bill had taught him the things his own father took for granted he would know by the first time they hunted—the handling of guns, dogs, himself.

Now his uncle was sleeping it off back at the motel with the other dog in his bed, while Bronk got the birds they would share with both families. Of course, if his uncle had been with him, he wouldn't have shot the one in the water. You were supposed to wait until they took flight—that was sporting. But he had better things to do than wait out a bunch of birds. Besides, better to get it over with. What chance did they have against his gun, anyway? What was sporting about an expert shot with repeating shotguns?

Should have brought both dogs, he thought again, as he settled the first, then the second and third bird beside him. Damn things were so big. They'd be way over limit. Even counting them as his uncle's share too, which he'd have to make sure to get hidden before he went back to the motel. Damn game wardens. Once they'd even taken the guns. His uncle and father still laughed about that time. Four hundred dollars in guns and they'd had to pay a fine too. Now his father had given up going out with the two of them. He was flying into Canada with other successful businessmen, and the annual fall bird hunting had turned into a trip Bronk took with his uncle Bill. Just because he didn't want to go into the business. Or maybe because of that thing with the fraternity, getting kicked out of school. Hell, it was just a joke. Not his fault he was the only one got caught. Everyone else had jumped off the truck and run when they saw the driver turn back from the store he was delivering to. But Bronk had just stood there, drunk and curious. Alfie'd almost had a hold on the keg. A linebacker and beefed up for the fall, he would've made it if Bronk had just rolled it into his arms the way they'd planned. But Bronk had frozen, like one of the geese, curious as the driver panted up to their sides and grabbed him like a twelve-year-old on his way out of the store with candy stuffed down his pants. Alfie ran. He remembered thinking, So this is what happens. The cops came and booked him and took away his belt, and the small-town jail cell settled into premature night around him. When his father arrived the next day, his face wore disbelief, as if he'd just learned of a fatal disease. "You asshole," he said. "Why didn't you run?"

There were five geese surrounding him in the blind, each one with the same dull staring eye, the wide yellow bill, and the blooms of blood in the breast that it wore like medals. He arranged the feet of the birds neatly. They would have goose for Thanksgiving. He would bring the birds, and everyone would be surprised and happy. His father would call his friends to come over. He would proudly display his son's kill in the yard for everyone to see, bragging that there'd be no turkey this year. Bronk would drive way over the speed limit, Uncle Bill joking at his side, as they rushed in from western Nebraska to Omaha in time for his mother not to start the turkey on Thanksgiving morning. If the damn dog would hurry, they would make it by nightfall.

"Just a couple more," he advised the Lab, who lay panting half out of the water, his chin resting on top of the sixth bird he'd just deposited carefully on top of the others. The dog looked mournfully at the smooth bodies of the birds, beaded with water, shook its head halfheartedly to get the water off its face, and slipped back into the pond, to paddle slowly back to the white shapes bobbing like fat pillows.

Should have brought the other dog too, Bronk thought again. But then his uncle Bill would have woken up and wanted to come. He'd be clumsy and cursing with a hangover. He'd want to have the thermos filled and topped with schnapps before they left. And then smoking the whole time. Bronk knew the birds could smell it, hear his uncle's hoarse chuckle as he spun one joke or story after another, like casting a trout stream. He never tired, flicking them off like ashes from his endless cigarettes. Never any peace when his uncle got started. The only time he was silent was on the days Bronk's father refused to loan him money. Once it was to raise dogs, good ones he'd train and sell to the city men who hunted a few times a year but didn't want to raise and train their own, as his stepbrother was doing these days. Several years ago Uncle Bill'd given Bronk's family a Brittany spaniel as revenge or a joke—it was hard to tell. The dog was wonderfully bred, should have been the best in the field. Bronk's father hadn't wanted it, but Uncle Bill had been careful to arrive in town on a Sunday afternoon when all the kids were there and ready to fall in love with the new puppy. Bronk had to grin at that. The dog had been a cross for his father to bear. It was everywhere at once, chewing and tearing and pissing. No one had the time or knowledge to train it. His uncle could have, but Bronk's dad had already refused him money. The dog ended up at the Humane Society two years later. Bronk could still remember its defeated head bent to the small square of screen as it watched the house recede from the departing truck.

This whole trip Bronk had had to listen about the god-damn Dairy Queen franchise his uncle wanted to buy. They both knew his dad was going to turn him down, wouldn't even cosign on the loan.

"Just one more," he reminded the dog, as it deposited the eighth bird on the mound. Had he really killed all those? he wondered. How could that be? Maybe they died of fright. He smiled, planning to tell his uncle that when he opened the trunk of the car and lifted the rug he'd hide them under. "Just don't get caught" was the only advice his father had ever given him. That was why he'd waited at the beer truck. He figured, Why not?

Bronk watched the dog struggle at the far end of the pond. Damn, he wasn't going to drown, was he? Jesus, that'd be something. Tell his uncle he'd drowned his best hunting dog shooting over both their limits of Canadian honkers. His uncle would never believe his dog had drowned. He'd come closer to believing Bronk had shot him. He watched the dog tread water for a few minutes beside the last goose, which was beginning to sink. Dog had better get it pretty soon, or it'd be on the bottom with that other one. What the hell happened there? he wondered. Now there'd only be nine. Could've been ten. A record maybe. His father'd never shot anything close to that. Uncle Bill—he'd done seven once. But that was before, when he'd been younger. Hell, he hadn't even woken when Bronk had slipped out with both guns and ammunition. Good thing, too. Needed both to work the geese. Worth the risk. Uncle Bill never let another man touch his gun. It'd been his for as long as Bronk had been hunting with him.

But if the dog would hurry, he could be back to the motel before his uncle woke up, get the stuff packed, and have the car running when his uncle took the first piss of the day. He watched the dog take a halfhearted pull at the wing of the bird. Shit. He wasn't even trying to bring it back the way he should. Now what? Sure the dog was tired— weren't they all. Neither of them had had breakfast even. Not even a cup of coffee. But his uncle always said the black Lab had more heart than twenty dogs he'd ever seen. Now this. A wing, for Chrissakes. He watched it swim awkwardly, trying to tow the bird. "It'll take you all day," he said out loud, as the dog began to move sideways to get a better pull to the weight. Maybe he'd better call the dog, give it some encouragement. If he ruined the dog now, his uncle would kill him. First the Dairy Queen business, then this.

As Bronk stood up, he felt light-headed, dizzy, looking out across the brown and white fields harvested and down for the year. There were almost no trees in the sand hills, only an occasional break in the landscape with water and cottonwoods clustered around.

He felt as if he were suddenly at the top of the world, looking down and across it as if he were eight feet taller. And he could just reach across the pond and pluck the exhausted dog and the bird, wet and tattered like a stuffed toy left out in the rain, and drop them in the blind, pinched between the fingers of his huge hands. Years later, Bronk imagined, the family would treasure the pictures of him squatting with his gun in the yard surrounded by the nine dead geese and with the look of the serious hunter in his eyes.

"Come on," he called to the dog. "Come on, bring it home, boy." The Lab looked at Bronk, careful not to drop the sinking bird's wing as he floundered in the icy water. Bronk could see the disappointment in the dog's eyes as its nose dropped below the surface for the first time.

That Kind of Loving

I REMEMBER the heat of the gun as it swept over the bodies one more time, the way it burned the calves of my legs and made me clutch my child's head, harder into my covering arm, the floor.

I remember wondering if it was true, what she'd promised me: that it wouldn't hurt, that they would skip us, that we would rise up from the deadly bed to live with her, that she was sparing us and not the others, not the betrayers. I remember worrying that the blood and pieces of torn-off flesh would bounce up and over, that the bullets themselves would spray us accidentally. I wondered that her control could be so sure.

But it was. When the shooting stopped and I finally looked up, conscious that it could be my head exploding in a minute, there was only the body on the bed, some parent or another, and her with the gun, motioning for us, the child and me, to get up and go on to live our living with her.

I was assigned a room. I could visit with the dying patriarch, who couldn't speak. The child was taken elsewhere, and my fears lessened. Just the burning glance of heat across the backs of my legs like the sting of a whip.

Lady of Spain

THE FAMILY sat down to dinner. The drunk father thought he saw the porpoises swimming outside the glass wall. Certainly the ocean roared. Though it might have been another appliance of nature. The wind, rain—those were things he'd lost in the move. He'd looked hard in the back darkness of the van to see if there was anything else—dust, dry leaves. Anything for the silence.

He was wrong, though. When he drove inland, the city seemed like a cricket loud in his sleep, whose rhythm first went with his dreams, then didn't, and the jagged sound sawed his sleep in half. He would find himself awake on the freeway, gripping the wheel sternly like the head of the household.

When they arrived at the mall, everyone piled out like a visiting team, full of pep and determination. Mother, girl, and boy clutched their purses full of fifties and hundreds like equipment bags.

Hours later, fingers raw from rubbing surfaces of many different kinds of merchandise, muscles cramped from clutching bags, paper and plastic with and without handles, they lined up around the car. A Wagoneer, for inland mall trips. At the appointed click of the key in lock, the doors popped, and each person climbed in. What a team, they each thought. The family that had won the lottery drove back to the sea.

That evening, girl, boy, Mother all filed past Father seated in the family room overlooking the ocean, the inescapable water surging like a washing machine next to his chair behind the earplugs he'd put on. Each person dropped the shopping bags in his lap. The ones with handles or grippers earned the donor a big smile. Another hundred. Regular ones got the usual fifty. There was no cheating. They were a family.

That evening he folded each one, carefully creasing the paper along its original lines like a car map. This was the important part. To follow the formula for folding, in and out, back and forth. After each one was bent back into its natural resting shape, he stroked it gently. A reassuring pat, as for the family dog. Father liked the rough grain of paper as much as the smooth cream of plastic.

When the water shifted to rinse cycle, pounding itself on the rocks just below the house's perch, the sun fell to its knees behind the far lip of land and lost its eyesight. Then Father said okay, and the food appeared. The hands put it in a pretty shape. These hands were paid for. They'd do anything hands could. He knew that. They'd probably play catch with him if he said so.

The bay's half rind grinned open, and the blue water sat still. Held and then wrinkled like a serpent, the huge flat wedge of head yawned, and out came the porpoises.

Fat and gray. The hands took the glass away and gave him another. The porpoises skated the waves. Father fingered the molded plastic handle of the top bag. They'd paid cash for everything. They could return it tomorrow, but they never wanted to. It was easier for arms to carry it away.

Father looked at his family around the dining-room table. There wasn't an easy answer to his question. Each face had a storm in it. He wondered if it was going to rain. He doubted it. There was enough water here.

He missed *Wheel of Fortune*. The arms carried the television in, just as before. They didn't turn the wall on. The family liked the set that had been in the family for years. The arms balanced it carefully on two chairs at the end of the room where they could all see it. The family felt better when they saw the poor color and the antenna made out of a coat hanger Father had snipped apart with his wire shears and straightened. While they ate what the hand placed in front of them, the picture rolled in a familiar rhythm and settled. Green Pat Sajak spun the wheel to demonstrate the way it could be done if a person were lucky enough to get on the show.

Father felt sad when Vanna turned the letters. Porpoises. Grinning in the breakers. When the blue woman won a round, he felt a twinge like a brush of nettle along his leg.

A hand put a fresh glass by his chair. Tattinger. He liked that best. Vanna still smiled, her teeth blue. The words gradually appeared on the screen. Father wondered if he thought them first. The wine turned time around. Made it swim back and forth like the porpoises in front of the house.

But maybe it was reruns. He watched *Wheel* in Omaha, then again in Sea Cliff. Cable. Satellite. He had it all. Vanna and Pat hosting.

As he ate, he waited for the pause in the waves—the long hissing draw of breath, then the roll as they flung against the shore.

The ski jet lingered on its trolley outside the windows. The arms would come soon and blanket it with a canvas like a horse for the night. Its chrome and red enamel neck craned back at the sea like a brontosaurus watching the Ice Age curling over the hill behind it.

"Lady of Spain" the black man said and the audience clapped wildly. The girl and boy looked up, nodded to the prizes as they panned by. They owned one of each. The

china Dalmatians had been the first thing the family bought. Now the four china dogs patrolled the house like real ones. Maybe they were real. Father couldn't remember. He looked at Mother down the ten-foot slab of Carrara marble that served as their dining table. Maybe she'd remember.

The hand replaced her glass too. She stared at it as if she'd forgotten what it was for. Then she looked up, caught Father with the crystal at his lips, and understood. It was her Baccarat wineglass.

They smiled like Pat and Vanna at each other. In the background 50 million dollars flashed on and off—the neon sculpture they'd paid for in cash. Exactly what they'd won.

In her dreams, maybe they were his. Father saw the neon tubes uncoil and scale the stairs to their sleep. Sometimes they bit him, and fangs sank quick and deep into his arm. Sometimes they chased his legs. There weren't any hands to help in this sleep. Every time he tried to change things, the snakes got mad.

"Fine," he said. "Just fine." In the morning he lost his appetite. Everyone got concerned. The black bag appeared and checked his pulse. He'd paid for the bag. He wanted it just the way he remembered: peeling lizardy cowhide, scuffed and marred, the brass closings scratched in little runes. He wanted the bag to appear at dinner some night. So he could introduce it to the *Wheel* contestants.

The ocean got louder as the family put itself to bed. Each top sheet turned back for want of anything else to do. A mint placed on the pillow. The remotes positioned dutifully next to the television clock. Set for the programs liked best.

Father kept his on the weather channel. He watched almost all night long as weather rolled in from across the nation. It made him feel patriotic. He called his congressman and gave him money.

Outside the bedroom, windows stretched like a passenger train along the cliffs. The porpoises kept busy. Night and day—they didn't know which they preferred.

Father listened to a show tune from their watery throats. "Lady of Spain, I adore you. Lady of Spain, I loove youuu." They sang over and over and over.

Home Video

THIS IS A TRUE STORY. A story of forgiveness. A man with bread-crumb sins. A woman who pecks them out of sight. Another woman who can stay hungry for a long time.

In California the beach was crowded with water. That was one thing she saw, while the home video hummed along, an excursion of bad focus and poor judgment. She tried to pick out the background, the missing spaces. An exercise, looking at the air around the bodies on the beach. In the background of one scene she thought she could see a dark wedge of fin in the water, accusing her, and wondered if his family had seen it as they splashed in the surf. The grown children like porpoises, diving and breaching the waves, while the shark watched farther out. Or was it watching her? Maybe it was her fish. In the living room of his house it could watch what she was doing where she wasn't supposed to be.

When the movie ended, he put them away, tucked the children and grandchildren back in their black plastic.

"Well, that was some vacation, I guess," he said.

She watched him go into the kitchen and heard the unsticking of refrigerator rubber.

"Want anything?" he called. But she'd given her tongue to the fish, so she just shook her head.

"What?" he called. He worried at fifty-five that he was losing his hearing. Watched his head fall apart in the sink every morning. Very little dignity left to a man, he decided one day and got her.

Actually, she was the third in five years, but his head had been going for so long that it collapsed in slow motion like big game shot on television. He saw the elephant fold itself up and said, "There I go."

When he didn't hear from her in the living room, he forgot her. He was eating. His wife did the same thing. Forgetting to talk. Women. He liked them. But he had to remind himself to remember them. His wife knew this about him and had posted pictures of the family all over the house like army regulations.

While he spread mayonnaise, her face above the counter, surrounded by grandchildren blossoming in the garden, told him to put the lid on the jar. In a chorus: "Put the jar in the fridge." He did as he was told. Closed the sandwich like a thick book and put it on a plate to catch the crumbs. Her cartoon on the fridge eyed him: "Napkin."

He stopped at the bar in the den. "Drink?" he called to her. This time he avoided the hearing test and poured her what she liked. He knew it wasn't what the wife liked. In the den he was surrounded by his I'm-important pictures. Early on they'd decided that and saved them while he made money. In none of these pictures was he alone. That was the whole point. I'm-important pictures needed the other person in a supporting actor role: the guide when he caught the trophy fish, the governor when he got the award, the president when he gave the dollars. This was a room he didn't have to visit much. He felt good just knowing it was there.

Carrying the two drinks with the plate balanced on top, he walked back to where she lay half-naked on his wife's designer fabric couch. There were two in the room. The girl automatically took the best. He got to spill himself there and worry about cleaning it later, maybe not at all. It gave the wife something to think about.

Pumping away with his trousers and shorts hanging on one ankle like a nasty little dog. He kept trying to kick them off, which she thought was some wild variation he'd gained over the years. He saw this and kicked harder. The pants hung on. He bucked and kicked like a kangaroo in her pouch. He was thigh deep in her. She had a tunnel of love he tried to widen and channel through. She was barely big enough. He knew that and pounded his stake. "She's mine," he claimed on the sign. "Mine." And he baptized his wife's rose sofa.

"Well, here we are," he said lowering drinks and sandwich. She sat up, eyeing the food greedily. On the end tables his children's families gathered to watch him. How did he have so many people in his life? he wondered. It had surprised him how easy it all was. He wasn't that surprised anymore, though. He'd gotten used to doing a thing and liking it.

Like the girl here. He handed her half the sandwich and watched the dripping of tomato and mayo bloody the cream carpet. His wife would believe he'd done it. He wished he'd known she was going to eat. He wanted the whole thing himself. He reached over and cupped a breast, a fine young one. Well, there. And fingered the nipple like an ignition button on a powerful boat.

She put down the sandwich half and lay back, glad. When she closed her eyes, his fingers ran her like a keyboard. "Here, here," they called, as if there were sharks in the water.

She whispered, "Let's go to bed." He shoved the food aside and lifted her. He was glad to be lifting someone. And up the stairs they went, their clothes a tidal pool on the living room carpet when the pictures climbed down and waded through.

In the wife's bed she made up for the home movies. Seven married pictures were ringing the bed. She entered like a bull. She hooked him. She enjoyed the audience rooting for the wife. She'd been an underdog. It was a good fit.

He liked it best here. He felt the stamp of approval on the room as he thrust in and out. He'd never had it so good. He was going to keep it up for years after this. He could plan the addition on the house while he stayed hard. He never came till he was tired.

Lots of windows. A little room for I'm-important and we're-a-family. His wife might want to post their names on a clever plaque the way she had done at the cabin. That was nice. So he didn't forget.

Underneath him the girl was happy. She thought this meant he liked her better. She smiled, and he thought it was for him, but he was wrong: it was for the wife watching from the walls. The wife smiled. She thought it was because he was there in the picture with the family. She was wrong: it was because it was her house.

The husband had the roof on by the time he finished. He felt young enough to go again. Maybe he'd buy a new boat for the kids to water-ski behind at the cabin. Or maybe he'd take the family to California again. It was fine except for the sharks. They never came in close enough to bother you, though.

He'd take this girl to Las Vegas. Show her off, give her some fun. He was happy. Everyone was smiling. The house sang with joy.

Cupid

LESLIE AND FRANK are parked right outside the museum. The air and the streets are moist and dark, springlike, although it is too early for winter to be over. All day the change in weather has pulled people from their houses onto the sidewalks, bewildered, their jackets open. At dusk it has begun to drizzle lightly, just enough to bring the good dirt smell up out of the ground temporarily.

Leslie knows. She spent the afternoon with Frank, walking around, talking about books and his life. He is a famous poet visiting, the star. Though now his hair is gray, his face lined, he is still a beautiful boy. The early clear looks that drew men and women alike to him are lingering there, smudging his face with a sense of what is gone. To see him now, Leslie thinks, is to feel loss, regret.

Frank is saying, "And Amal gave me this—pure stuff. He always has good drugs." She watches as he pries the lid of the medicine vial off.

"Tennessee Williams," Leslie says, and he laughs. He is feeling loose now.

They have stopped at a liquor store in a poorer neighborhood where he felt confident he could get a pint of Jack

Daniels in a paper bag. He wanted the bag to fit exactly with just enough to twist around the top. He wanted it to look right when he drank on stage that night. He'd insisted she go in with him.

She felt his eyes splash like oil on her legs as he walked in behind her. She watched him lick his lips as the drunks around them savored her short tight black leather skirt, studded belt, blouse open to show she had no bra on. She felt Frank's step lighten and rise as he searched the store longer than he had to, while she was positioned like a package he'd checked at the counter. She felt the bee hum of the men as they pulled wadded dollars from their filthy jeans and followed her gold chain all the way down the dark crevice where it disappeared between the curves of her breasts. She brushed their sound away from her face with the back of her hand.

On the way to the car, Frank had hugged her. Inside, they each took a quick hit from the bottle. Leslie knew he was going to kiss her. It was only a matter of time. She'd felt slightly betrayed when she found herself pulling the black leather out of the closet, slipping on the dark stockings, the black spike heels, as if they'd always had this appointment. She was too old to feel safe in this outfit anymore. She wasn't afraid enough when he looked at her.

Instead, Leslie watches the theatergoers, hand in hand, walking up the steps and entering the church huge glass doors. The museum, which only saves twentieth-century art, shares the structure, which, like municipal buildings, jails, courthouses, and libraries, seems designed to make people seem small, transient.

Next to her in the car, Frank is busy doing mysterious things. Once he reaches over and changes the radio station to hard rock. Leslie remembers his role with some of the popular bands of the sixties. His was a presence—beautiful, additional. Everyone had wanted him then. She remembers seeing him in a film, how he took your breath away, then gave it back in a new language. It hurt to see him leave the stage—a real physical thing she stored inside until this moment of him next to her in the dark of the car as he prepares his drugs.

"Have you ever tried this?" Frank asks.

When Leslie shakes her head, he takes the rolled dollar bill and places it a hair above the white powder in the vial cap. The only noise is a long breathy sigh. Then he does the other nostril and leans back, closing his eyes for a minute while his head rests on the seat. "Amal's right. S'good. Perfect."

She doesn't want to appear too eager, so she waits until he opens his eyes and offers her the rolled dollar. She knows how to do it. She's seen it in movies over and over. She's even been offered some before. But she's never done it, never trusted herself. Tonight with the whisper of leather on her arms and thighs, with the damp before-spring air and the coming lights and performance she'll watch, she feels the old ground inside of her breaking up.

At first Leslie feels nothing. She's done it slowly so as not to make a mistake and blow the powder into the car or knock it over. She's seen that in a movie too and heard the advice that if you go slow with something new, you'll look as if you know what you're doing. She believes it.

Then it hits her. Not like a train, not as she expects, but as if a platform she's been standing on is slowly rising. And the dark ground inside her that she's always afraid of softening, crumbling, becomes a sheet of marble. The world gets flat and interesting, very bright and pure. She knows almost everything.

When they get out of the car, they hold hands until the steps. Then he adjusts the scarf he wears around the collar of his upturned sports coat, checks the weight of the pint in his pocket, and fixes the leather case of poems under his arm. "How do I look?" Frank asks.

Leslie smiles and nods. He smiles and says, "Later. Oh, and don't say anything to Amal. I was supposed to save him some." All her friends like her confidence, admire the black leather, her legs. In the bathroom in front of the mirror she opens her blouse another button.

After Frank's performance they get lost trying to find his hotel. When his hand first slides inside her blouse, she slows down and laughs uncomfortably. It should feel good.

Leslie rubs his thigh tentatively, thinking that some response is required. It would seem rude of her, otherwise. He feels encouraged and sticks his hand up her skirt. She squirms as his fingernails scratch at her panty hose.

When they find the hotel room, Frank immediately strips. Leslie sits on the bed. It is such a small room, and when he turns on the television without sound so they'll have some light, she feels disappointed.

She doesn't want him to kiss her. The drug makes that much clear. What he wants is her sucking on him and, more important, him sucking on her. He rummages through her clothes like a bear in garbage, testing pieces and places for sweetness, for appealing tastes. Then he spreads her legs so far they ache, and he shoves his face in her. Later Leslie sucks on him for an hour, while Frank moans and never comes.

While she dresses, he keeps telling her, "Find someone who loves you. Find someone tomorrow who loves you."

She can't see how to tell him that's impossible, so she just keeps agreeing. Actually, on her way home she does try to think of someone to love her, but it doesn't seem as though there's anyone around. She goes through everyone, including married friends. "I'm going to call and check on you in the morning, okay?" he'd said. "I want to get a progress report."

When Frank calls the next day, it is early afternoon. "Did you do what I told you to do?"

"I'm looking," Leslie tells him, as she adds the drug to the list of things she can't do again. It makes everything too possible. She has to.

Later she receives a book of Frank's poems, like the one she already has. He has inscribed it to her. Leslie thinks of how at one point in their sex, he had rushed to the bathroom, and she could hear him groaning in pain as he urinated. "I have a problem," he'd said when he returned. "It hurts. It's not contagious—don't worry."

Working Their Betrayals
(To Keep Us Alive)

DOWN AT THE STORE they rock on the front porch, hands deep in the open sides of their overalls, fingering thoughtfully while I pass by, walking as fast and tight as I can. I can feel their eyes catch my smell, sniff it down between my legs. They come to greet me like dogs, those eyes nosing the hem of my dress up the bare inside of my leg, the streak of wet cool to my skin they shove it up to, and I feel the hardness press in like a cup, like a hand they cup me into, bend me over and pour. They'd like to pour me out, liquid and creamy on their fingers, on their hard fingers sliding the ridges, the nibs of flesh up inside. The men sit dreamy as turtles, as snakes, in the heat. They are stretched and lost as I walk fast and tight by, no pitcher they pour out of today.

I work my escape. In a block they lose track and drop back uninterested as dogs, shuffle back to the shade of the porch in front of the store, where men lean back in chairs, hands shoved deep and dreamy into the unbuttoned sides of their overalls. Someone goes for a Coke—gets up stiff with looking and waiting, pulls the front of his pants down, and turns, the heavy work boots a soft *clump-clump* on the floor, and all I can see is his back eaten by the darkness of the door-way.

Down the street they wait inside other doorways, half-shadows bulging slighting into the screens, silent. These men never speak to me from their tiny paint-peeling houses, the implement-store fronts, the diner where they sit at tables by the long front window, coffee cooling into their hands as they speculate on me. I am mined for the hard bursts of nipples I shiver back from the thin cotton front of my dress. They lose nothing here against all the losses they have suffered. Expert, they finger those nipples, put their eyes like tight buds of lips against them and tease, suck the brown hardness like tobacco, and gradually their teeth eat sweet sweet peas they think will pop their thin skins and roll into their waiting mouths. I can smell the coffee and nicotine-stained breath, the fog rising onto me, over me, but I can't stop breathing. It comes inside like something I ate, bad, tasting bad, and falls into my stomach. The smell of it works back and forth, rubbing me raw with its broken glass edges. I walk on. Their eyes drop back to the ringed, rubbed table. One of them takes his forearm and slowly wipes at a cloudy spot before him. When I look back, the sunlight sheets the window blank.

Finally I am there, the unpainted wood dried gray, sep-arating from itself, pulled apart by gravity of such feelings I don't know, the porch empty. I know where he is. I am tired as I climb the steps, careful of the slope threatening to spill me off if I'm not careful. I could go away, I could go to the damp hot woods, I could keep walking, but I don't. My hand, familiar to this act, finds the knob in spite of me and gently pulls the screen door's surprising lightness, the squeak I wish to hush, always to hush from him. Like a tiny wire, it runs me swiftly on its sound to where he waits in the smell of exhaustion and urgency and the low lazy buzz of flies over the days' old food, the glass sticky with whiskey and Coke, which he makes me drink. I see the flies clearly, as one dips an antenna over the lip expectantly. And behind this I feel the hum of him, which I hear and don't hear, in the back room, door ajar, all dark and expectant in its heat, its smell.

I walk quietly, yet he hears me. I slide sideways into the room, don't even disturb the door, but he is always awake, like a fish swimming uselessly back and forth against the glass that walls the water it would not break out of. I think I see his eyes, two shiny animals in the corner, on the low hard bed. Today there is something else, unexpected, the way he holds the thick fluted Coke bottle, but familiar, the way it glints an arrow of light into my belly and his square silver belt buckle clinks against the glass as he pulls me toward it, into the pale cradle of skin, glowing with the dim green light from the window behind him, thick with lilac and verbena dropping sickly and sweet onto the bed around him.

See the Pyramids

IT WAS A SUMMER when the greenness wore off, when she woke up not as hot and sweaty as when she'd fallen asleep, but one day was still just like another. Cleaning the glasses and bottles from beside the bed took such effort that she only briefly looked at the tiny moth flattened on the water in the orange plastic glass. Other summers, this would have been of interest.

Now she tried to endure the time it took to get to sleep, to cool off so she could cover herself with her comforter. Though it was too hot, she had gotten so she couldn't dream without the familiar wrap of her comforter. She even dreamed of comforters. Everyone had a preference. Quilted, with little tufts of yarn like laziness sticking out. Not reversible. Hers was. Pattern or not. Or they chose heavy wool squares. Too scratchy. Hers was smooth, with the smooth warm sunset to glide a hand over her skin, oranges and yellows to blend. Nothing blue or wet about it.

This was the summer when it all wore off. She moved. She stopped paying bills. She dyed her hair red and then let it grow out, slow as tomatoes ripening. The roots darkened and spread their color upward, like a second hand in a long sweep of time. It seemed to her that summer and heat were just ahead of her and just behind her.

It scared her, this lack of interest. She planted things and let them die in the heat. Some never made it out of the cardboard box beside the back door. The African daisy, in a final burst of effort, put out its blossom and dried stiff as wood in the heat. Only the coralbells, which she'd bought because she'd never liked them, remained delicate and green.

At night the dreams were hurried and confused. By dawn they would slither slow as snakes across the floor—whole pools of snakes, familiar and unfamiliar outside a door. She tried to turn them over to catch the other side. For once she wasn't afraid of them. They left reluctant to the touch of her foot. She was careful not to step on any.

When the cat sprang across her bed to the dresser, she opened her eyes to see it perched on the edge, staring not at her but at the blank white wall. She turned over, whispering, "Edgar, Edgar." Later it slept silent as dust in the windowsill.

One day, the hottest of the summer, she went out to ride her horse, choosing the hottest hour to take him to a field, where she beat him. When he was wet all over, she brought him back to the cool dark indoor arena and comforted him. She never did this again. He watched her from a wiser distance. She would always be sorry.

A man who made love to her in the winter and disappeared wrote her a letter. She wanted to feel more about it, his apology. In her dreams she still loved him. When she saw him, she had nothing to say. He talked about his discoveries, his life, as if about a novel he were were enjoying. She watched him as if he were an actor on the screen. When it was over, she asked, "What will it be like now?" He looked at her as if she had awakened him from a dream, then away, across the parking lot, and shrugged his shoulders.

A friend returned from Ireland, bringing a gift for her house: an antique brass plate a foot long, with intricately cut-out designs of birds and hearts and, in the middle, the keyhole. "For your door," he explained. She hung it on the tiny nail over her kitchen calendar. It fit over the picture of July, a photo of a man on the beach in old-fashioned clothing, facing the ocean. Then only his shadow, cramped by the angle of the sun, showed fully—and a hand holding a stick and parts of bare feet and legs. She looked through the keyhole, but, large as it was, it showed only the darkness of a shoulder and gray sky.

Side Road

I HAVE PULLED the semi sideways, swung it across the road
and into the cleared area – not a pasture or field, more a wide
graveled place where I would park it, except that is not what I
am doing. I am racing across the top of it. You have to get this
part in your mind. I may have a gun, and I may not. Anyway,
it's not important. I am chasing and being chased by them.

That's what you need to know. I have driven the round
trip south in two and a half days. Hurrying, I can't remember why, but it's there. Some need and a feeling of trying to
bring a thing off that I could laugh about later: the trip. I feel
that I have walked, run, cycled, and now it turns out I drove
the semi. Only now I am stopped here, and we are racing
around the truck.

Enough, I say and let myself go with them, though this
part isn't in the picture.

The next scene is in a place that is nearly not one. It lacks
even the distinctiveness of the not-a-pasture-but-gravel
place I parked the truck in. I see the walls and don't – you
know how that is: the gray silver darkness of curved ceiling
and stuff that could be cave and could be someone's idea of
movie interior. The color is important because although the
first part was daytime, this section is night, and it's certainly

true that we're all white and pale and plainly not even seductively dressed. The emphasis is on the packages of red they are handling and what is to happen in a moment.

They talk to me, these men, testing me verbally, with that hesitant teasing that is so offhand that you understand you really have no power here. So I keep watching what they are doing with their hands. Some kind of assembly line. And something they are halfhearted about wanting me to see, yet I discover in a moment they are just waiting for the issue of timing, like everything else. My eyes in the smoky light are of course drawn to the red, which is deep and rich like fresh livers only not that dark. Certainly the consistency is true. Fresh, raw, red, red livers, huge ones. Something says that these are human. Not from cows, which they would seem to be from their size, but parts of humans. Butchered, yes. And the dawning of that hits simultaneously with the matter-of-factness with which the men are handling them, each in its heavy plastic bag, clear, of course, so it looks like something on its way to the freezer in an ordinary kitchen. Did I say this was a kitchen? Well, it's not.

There is a tone here, cajoling and threatening, like the color of the place and us and then the too red meat. But not meat, not the way you think of steak. This is organ, something intimate red, something closer, something deeper, and there is a mounting feeling that this might be a place you could get hurt in. But not quite that—more something that will be witnessed here, that you might not recover from, something awful, something you will later describe with fear, as hell.

Did I say that the place was crowded with people? Genderless. As in the lightness of their skin and clothing, the odd silver gray of the walls and floor—"porch gray" I would call it, though I can't really say I actually noticed it. This is the kind of detail you pull from nothing except what had to be because it couldn't be anything else.

Whether I am arguing with him or not, who can say now. It all happens so fast at this point. He turns and throws some of the meat's redness at them, and the room is a frenzy of feeding. The meat spurts and blood flies as if a bomb had exploded inside the bag, but the bag wasn't there. They are feeding on the meat and on one another or on someone as hapless as me, tearing pieces of flesh and the flood of red, only the spatter is the effect—and the slash of teeth and tearing claws and mostly the swirl and sprawl and knot of bodies, like fish feeding in a frenzy. Nothing mammalian. Not wolves attacking a deer on ice. That's too nearly what we would be like. No, this is another species, alien. These figures change forms, as if the arms and legs were merely costuming for the sharp teeth and jaws and the blood that was to be handled. Not just sucked and licked but bathed in, rubbed on like elixir. And the man next to me, who could have put his hand in my back and shoved me into their midst on the floor, did not.

I understand that this is by way of demonstration and that what he is about is the packaging, the meat. My being human or not is of no concern to him. There is no way out of this place.

The truck pulled slantwise onto the clearing shoulder and my plans for the round trip are what used to be. My thoughts are, for once, empty. It is the sweat of revulsion, of having seen something I was not supposed to see, of having come too far this time.

Time Only Adds to
the Blame

SEE, THE PROBLEM starts with the body. There isn't one. Not that we can see. So how can it be any different? Like James Dean or Jim Morrison. They must still be alive somewhere. Mother arrives from South Carolina retirement. First thing she asks, "Where is it?" We'd been all through that on the phone. But she's still asking two days later as she boards the plane back South.

"It's gone," we say. "You wouldn't have liked it anyway." The stewardess glances at us like *we* killed her. I shake my head and buckle mother in, noticing the drip of lunch. Was it there before the service? I can't remember and try to pick its scab off her good black linen. The dress looks suspiciously like part of the yellow and black mother'd worn to my wedding a month before. A giant bumblebee in distress.

The body hadn't been there either. "Don't tell Mother I'm broke," the body had urged.

"Well, it's pretty obvious you're not here." I'd been miffed, with the flowers she was supposed to carry down the aisle stinking up the house already. It was four hours till the church, and for once I was supposed to be the star attraction.

"I can't help it. You understand." I didn't.

"And then when he had to drop out of the campaign – and those crazy LaRouche people – I didn't get my money. Do you see?"

"Okay." It was the only thing I could think of – that and a heavy sigh to let her know where things really stood. We never told the truth. That was the big thing for us. "You can do anything you want, but don't you step on my blue suede shoes." Lying had become the only way we could all be nice to one another anymore.

Then there was the unmistakable clink of glass against the receiver. Later I would see that it could have been the whole bottle too. She bulk-ordered them from the liquor store down the street. And like an apology for the sound – another lie we laid like a piece of railroad track all the way between her town and mine with a contract stating, No one rides this train – she said, "Oh, and your present's coming."

It was always coming. I wanted to tell her that the only resurrection happened in April, and you had to go to church for that one. But the present was a lie we knew so well it had come to stand as a code: Saying it makes it true. I've given you the antique garnets my husband got from a client, a hand-knitted sweater from Ireland, the silver bracelet my artist friend made.

I even thanked her.

"If I'd only seen the body . . ." Mother smooths the black linen, and I try to imagine the yellow striped jacket it should have over it. A highway sign: DANGER. I want to take those big hands with the big oval fingernails someone has painted a bloody red and squeeze them too tightly. Even with the knobs and turns of arthritis, they hold power and cruelty. They can hurt us again.

"There is *no* body." I say.

Her fingers test the metal buckle of the seat belt for sharpness like a knife blade. The rims of her eyes moisten, and her pupils harden against it. "Of course there is."

She's fading into a better place, I realize, as I put my cheek dutifully against hers. To touch her bare skin gives me a shock, like the numbing buzz on the electric fence on the day the plastic grip split and current leaked into my closed hand. The body had laughed. My arm had savored the sting all afternoon. Neither of us told that the fence was broken.

"Okay, Mother," I say, backing down the aisle. She looks at me with sudden hate, as if she's sorry that I'm not the body.

Once in the terminal, I want to run back through the boarding gate and tell her it wasn't my idea. I wasn't even going to invite her to the wedding. The body made me do it.

In the following weeks, we all came to see what a mistake it was, not to have tried harder for it. We are like the losing team who has to face the home crowd. We came back without a body, nothing to put in the showcase. Although we'd brought cameras, no one had the heart for pictures. What would we say—"Here we are at her funeral, but since we couldn't come up with a body, we had a memorial service instead, so here we are"?

First we went to the funeral home and got in the coffin elevator. We had to stand in a row. It took five of us upright to equal one body flat.

I'm always the joker. My father's the same way. He had a laughing fit right in the middle of my baptism. I had to think of bad things. It was his idea to begin with: "Just to keep Mother quiet." She'd had an attack of religion and had seen to it that I went through confirmation in the Methodist church. As a senior in high school, I was the oldest kid there. The minister got tired of my questions, but he let me finish anyway. He must've known I didn't believe in God. But it turned out they'd never had me baptized. The body had been. She joined the church on time too. She was like that—a step ahead of me.

As we stand on the third floor of that Chicago mansion

turned funeral home, looking at the boxes and urns on the gray metal shelving, I want to make a joke. I work at pulling the corners of my mouth down although they lift like helium balloons as soon as they can. Like the day mother told me that Gram had cancer. I had to turn my back so she couldn't see the dazzle of teeth. She must've thought I was going to cry. In our family, another part of the code: You cry, you cry alone. It's like a lie, I guess. But I'm not in danger usually.

Mostly I'm curious. I can hardly concentrate on the containers tricked up to look like something ordinary you'd use to store cigars or jewelry or flour. In the gloom around us sit the coffins. They hunch like dogs waiting on the porch for the master to come home. They sparkle like rows of new cars in those vast suburban dealerships. I want to walk up and down the rows, rubbing my hand over all the shiny surfaces. Here is something that says death. I feel cheated by the stupid canisters.

The body's daughter will have to come back and choose, we decide. For all our casualness, we are too shocked to pin it down. Burned. "We don't even have a body," we each protest silently. "Ashes" doesn't come up. We can't make that conversion. It's like a problem in metrics.

The body's ex-husband drives us from building to building, to pick up forms and releases, yet she isn't ever seen anywhere. Finally, on the street in front of a Travelodge he drops his teenaged daughter who is wearing a shabby blue-gray knit top and skirt, dirty, sizes too big for her. I want to yell at him, "What's this?" But we just go inside and get her a room.

All afternoon he has chain-smoked, the car's air conditioning barely huffing to cool the caustic summer heat. I crank open a window and look at the buildings he likes or doesn't like. Chicago architecture has become personal—he owns it somehow. I find myself liking the ones he hates, violently liking them. I could kill him I like them so much.

We eat because we have nothing to do. We're afraid to drink, which is what we should do. Whenever we lift a glass or imagine the familiar bite of liquor on our tongues, we glance guiltily around at the others. We have to do this. We're afraid of the body.

That's what we should tell Mother: "You're so brave, you go find it." She doesn't have to stop herself from wanting a drink. Secretly, when we've exhausted each other and are back in our separate rooms, I want to order liquor, all kinds. I want to drown in it. Get singing-loud drunk, go rouse them up, and have a good look at it. The body. We could all sit close, eat popcorn, and slouch low in our seats when the scary parts come on. As it is, we lie sober and alone in our beds. I leave the light on, though my new husband sleeps like a hand along the edge of my body. "What does he know?" I ask the face in the television I watch without sound. Motions. That's all I want. Not the voices. There's too much to say already.

Sometime in the night, whether asleep or awake—what difference does it make?—I decide two things:

1. My sister is not dead.
2. If she is, he killed her.

What would you do? Mother knows. She almost says it out loud. I think I can see her jail-stripe yellow and black jacket peeking out of her suitcase like a trapped animal, when I pick her up for the service.

As we drive over, she asks, "Is the body going to be at the church?"

Taxi rides for three blocks. They think we're crazy, so we overtip them as an admission of guilt. "Yes, it's true," our fingers clutching the extra bills say. "You guessed it, bud."

Inside, there's the usual: architecture we can all agree on. Tastefully, baroquely ornate. How could she leave this? I ask myself. She couldn't. See, the answer is simple. Irresistible.

Somebody's dead, I caution myself. We rise and kneel and rise and kneel. But I'm lucky. I just had a wedding with this religion, so I know how to pull the kneeler out, get up and down without snagging stockings or tumbling headlong into the pew in front of me.

Abraham Lincoln used to come here to worship. Just the place for the body. Probably way out of our league. I glance both ways down the row of us. We're dressed all wrong. Too grim. Black. You don't wear black anymore. I've got blue on. Doesn't that count for something?

Mother looks around her, skepticism in those hard blue eyes. Her hands tremble with anger as she grabs a hymnal, as if to say, "That same damn song." She thinks we've hidden her daughter, that she's away with a man secretly. "How do you know it's her?" she asked on the phone.

"He identified her."

"Oh, him," she scoffed.

While the minister, who is too young, talks about things, I have a disturbing sight: the body is going up the heavenly stairs. She wouldn't do anything unladylike, so the ladder'd be out. And leading her is Our Lord Jesus Christ. She looks pretty good, I notice, for someone who's just starved to death. "That's what happens when you drink instead of eat," I want to yell at her. But she looks fine, so who am I to talk? Then she glances over her shoulder with this smug look—self-satisfied, that's it—a smirk. "I'm still way ahead of you," it says. Right there she turns, and, without tripping on the sheer robes of grace, she is gone, waving goodbye once, like Miss America opening a shopping mall.

Does that mean there's a body? I cry harder, knowing she's got something I don't.

There are times at the reception tea, with real china cups, pâté, and cucumber canapés, when I wish real hard for that body. Oh, I do wish. I want it there just the way they found it: shrunken pygmy-small and naked. I want it to look like an

Egyptian mummy fresh out of storage. I want all those women who want the body to get it. I want to grab their restless, greedy hands and shove them onto her skeleton-hard skin. "Here it is," I want to say to them. "Now you know."

Instead, we comfort them. I even promise to return the crystal bowl one lady loaned the body two years before. She's so drunk, she won't remember. The man who gives the eulogy is drunk too. And the ex-governor and her ex-husband. Everyone has had a drink but us. How fair can this be?

Only Mother, in her black dress like a lethal can of spray paint, receives comfort from her own words. No one asks her a thing. She gets to talk undisturbed, while the rest of us look at the pickets of lies growing around the table she sits at.

I notice a pattern in our conversations:

1. They ask how I'm feeling. "You know . . ." I say.
2. They want the body, the chalk mark on the rug like in the movies.
3. They want to tell how long it's been since they said or did something with her. A badge of honesty. Their Girl Scout eyes say, "This is an apology."
4. Like amateur coroners, they come back to the body. Cause of death. Exact. C of D. I find myself smiling too often now, my mouth like a person belching.

There is the matter of her Lake Shore condo. The windows overlooking the basin, where the moored sailboats bob and tug like geese, are so clouded with dirt, even the sunlight filters brown over the wrecked living room. But I don't tell them details: the feces stuck to the sink, toilet, floor, cabinet, sheet, wall, rug, because she forgets how to take care of herself. Or won't.

I give them Camille, Portia Faces Life, Madame Bovary— "I have always depended on the kindness of strangers." "You can't even trust your own family," my eyes tell them, as my mouth rides up and down. I can't give them a body, and that's what they came for. They'll leave something behind, a donation to the church, but first they have to be sure there's been a crime. Murder. Suicide. Death.

Instead, they leave hours later, pausing to look around the bare linoleum floor of the church parlor with dissatisfaction on their faces.

"I didn't even like her," says a woman who is the last to leave. She is lingering by an embarrassingly large bouquet of orange flowers in the center of the room. "This is mine." She points at the silver bowl and the loud arrangement. "I want it back. I only did it because his new wife's my friend. Like I said, I couldn't stand her. She cursed me all the way across a restaurant one night."

The orange stands out because the body hated it. We order white flowers for the reception. White is correct. We know that. White calla lilies. And we order: *no* new wife. But she comes anyway, with her caterer and orange-flower friend.

I find myself saying a little prayer, asking only that the fetid breath of the body loose itself on any orange flowers in the room. Just once. Just once. But there's no miracle.

After the reception the sisters go to the bathroom to repair makeup. I am talking to them through the gray metal door of the stall. When I come out, though, I'm alone. They've all left, forgotten me. It's the loneliest feeling, see. Though I can hear their voices in the hall outside, I know they've forgotten me. I stand and stare into the mirror mounted on the gray tile wall. Under the fluorescent light I look old enough to be the oldest now.

"Goddamn it," I whisper to the mirror. She can't get away with this. But I just stand there, tears crowding out of my eyes, feeling sorry for me, because now I've got to be oldest and alone. This is worse than being tricked by those three husbands or having to earn my own living. I want to slap her face. "So where's the goddamn body," I whisper to her.

"Bring that goddamn body back here."

After the service the sisters take a taxi to the east-side police station to retrieve the body's jewelry. The station is new, clean, and efficient. The help is courteous. Things I notice about this excursion:

1. The trouble I have signing my name for the goods. We have agreed. I am the oldest. They step back for me when the desk person asks for a signature. Already they are pushing me out and ahead. From now on they'll be behind me. Well, good. Outside, I pull the taxi door open and climb in first. I thank her for that, wherever she is hiding.

2. We laugh all the way back to the hotel. Each of us wanting a drink to get the taste of jewelry or ash off our lips.

3. The satisfaction on her daughter's face when she opens the manila envelope with her mother's name on it and pulls out the gold bracelet set with sapphires and clips it on her own arm.

"It's just another lie," I tell my heart, as I watch Mother's plane rise out of the dull yellow Chicago sky. She'll be South in two hours. She can put her gangster clothes away.

Two years later we have almost stopped thinking about the clever marble jewel box the body's daughter picked out. As far as we know, it's waiting for us at the funeral home. There are a dozen excuses here. At first we torture each other weekly about it.

Father refuses to pay for anything. "When I die, throw my body in a ditch. I'm not spending a dime."

We think of buying land in a state none of us live in, keeping her on someone's mantel, in an attic or basement, on a lawn, in the lake, out to sea. Leaving her at the funeral home is a solution none of us imagines. That makes it the best one. The funeral home never contacts us. We don't contact them. It works out. Besides, they're the only ones who claim to have seen a body.

I Wonder Who's
Kissing Him Now

THE THREE WIDOWS entered separately and sat like periods along the blond curve of the pews. No one looked like Marilyn Monroe, but there was something pale and fair about each of them. The last, his daughter's age, was the finger on the trigger. Everyone blamed her, although the first, his high-school sweetheart, could have done it. He went to Nam, instead, to learn a trade.

The pallbearers entered in a clump of black suits and black hair, as if they had been chosen for their similarity. They glided down the aisle like blackbirds along a field of threshed corn, then descended and with the instinctive accuracy of a flock settled on the second row to the left. The family went center. They arrived with no distinction, as if some permanent separation, introduced by his act, must be noted, acknowledged.

The second widow he hadn't bothered to marry wanted to sit in the front row. Hers was the only voice that couldn't be heard, and it was the difficult thing to do. Her boyfriend, dressed in jeans and down vest, dragged her back at least behind the blackbirds: some decency in letting black go first. She wore red. She complained all day. Hers the voice that drove the car he would have liked to die in. But he got married instead.

Everywhere women were drying their eyes. There were so many widows that day, as if the only man in town had died. They came with children they claimed for his, though their husbands accompanied them.

The Vietnam captain sat in the back, just barely there with his wife and kids. They were divorced, so he was at a loss to comfort her—could only put on the suit, place the kids between them, and feel the hot breathing of his ex-lover behind him, her whanking on the Kleenex, and remember the time he went down on his knees in the parking lot of Dayton's just because the right song came on the radio. Something he remembered from the war. He'd never understood why the men weren't having a good time. He only learned to feel sorry for himself recently.

Across the room the women cried because they had opened their doors to the killer. Spread their legs because his sperm was harmless. He was gone before the little man got home. He was always urgent. The seduction was a clumsy affair, like being asked out for a Coke after school. No one got the wrong idea except him.

The men with red eyes were worried because the gun was being passed like a collection plate. They wouldn't let the women touch them, though that was the only touch they could stand. It was too much like skin on metal.

Widow number two watched the altar as if it was door number three. She could be on her way to the moon. The explosion of rock someone thought could take the place of glass in the altar window looked like a bricklayer's vision of God. Shards of weight. She knew that stuff wasn't taking her anywhere. She'd wanted some Bruce Springsteen instead of Jesus—Mick Jagger and the whole crew from the Rolling Stones. She hadn't bought the gun. She'd been on a self-improvement course when she met him, not married

him, left him. They'd been breaking up her marriage, putting the rags in the bags. She'd never intended to be on the
sucking end of the mop.

She had something to say. Her boyfriend kept his arm like
an iron sash weight across her shoulders and sang "Amazing Grace" with a fifties tempo. He was in a rock-and-roll
revival band, and the goofy haircut was part of the act. His
wife had also kicked him out. He could sympathize with
everybody. He wanted to be liked—it'd been a while.

Later a heavy redhead would call her friends, obsessed by
a Springsteen song and the look-alikes at the mall. He was
everywhere. Nothing died, she suddenly realized and
wondered if that meant her sister was still around. It made
her nervous that she couldn't throw anything away. Besides, there was the gun in her husband's glove compart-
ment. She tried to keep her hair dyed red and her smile
going. She had packed sex away after the kid was born, tucked it into the pockets of flesh she pulled on as if she were cold
all the time. Now her husband was working out and getting
calls from the young instructors.

Everyone wondered who else had dared to come. The
man who was suing him? Could you sue someone whose
body had no head? Could widow number three be taken to
court like a girl you met on *The Dating Game*?

Had the other five women he'd proposed to made the trip?

What if no one had ever accepted—would he still be here?
Was he just waiting for the scene to turn domestic so the
violence had a name?

When they wheeled in the closed coffin, everyone was
relieved, except widow number two. She'd grown fond of
the strange new head they'd fitted him with. She hadn't
gotten a chance to look for the bullet hole. His hair, she
would tell people, was that color and style after a shower:
swept back, straight. She kept asking people how big the
gun was.

Everyone else wanted to know what room in the house. It'd seemed like the kind of thing you'd do in the basement, but he was a man with no hobbies. A major failing. He tried out other people's the way you'd borrow a coat to go home from a party when the weather's changed: breeding horses, fucking women, taking drugs, watching MTV.

There was nothing to do in the basement. The skill saw was still sitting in its shrink-wrap.

The kitchen with the parrots? "I'd like one of those," the big redhead said to her friend.

The dining room, which widow two had blanked with white paint over wood paneling, baseboards, window frames, and ceiling? She'd wanted to do the wood floor, but he'd stopped her. What was the point of so much white?

Like part-time realtors, everyone wanted a floor plan. The place would be a steal now. They wondered if they could visit the scene of the crime.

Each person cried.

The body rolled by.

There was a stillness about it. The replacement head, the fake fingers stiff and fine—they'd had a manicure. The nails pointed so he could dig his way out if he had to. The hands like prosthetic devices crossed at the crotch, the only detail they inadvertently got right.

Everyone knew that the man with the head and the dumb shirt wasn't him. They'd tried to fool them with the wire-rim glasses, but it was such a childish thing, so obvious, no one was taken in. Like chickens in a yard with a dead dog, they all went up for their peek and peck.

Everyone just assumed that the box riding down the aisle on noiseless rollers, like a patient on its way to the X-ray room, was empty. At best, they'd shifted the artificial, not-him-maybe-some-other-guy body and put something else in there. So no one was watching but widow three, and she wasn't talking.

The woman who married them, buried him. The singer who sang, sang again, the same tentative voice, too reedy to be sure of itself – a fat girl who could drop it and go sexy if she tried. Did he screw her too?

They figured she was just part of the act. Why else would he bring them all to church? Any moment, he would walk down the aisle, grinning foolishly and proudly, and tell a funny story. They would all applaud and go downstairs dutifully to eat the Protestant funeral meal, on paper plates with plastic forks that snapped in the salad. Just another one of his tricks. With him, they knew, you always looked for double things. A riddle. If he said yes, he meant no. "That was his problem," widow two whispers to her boyfriend. Then he ends up in this goofy place.

The pallbearers rose suddenly, caught the draft, and sailed back down the aisle. Suddenly, the siblings no one recognized or cared about – where were they when he was playing Clue in the house that night? And the hated father, that voice that couldn't be replaced or duplicated except at the moment of gun in hand, killing.

Widow one, the cheerleader, looking her years with her kids in front of her – they walked alone, separate, like a piece of paper ripped in two, the ragged edge always showing. There was the son who took his dad's body because he was trying to kill it, even the tiny lock at the nape of the neck. He'd planned the funeral with a vengeance – something Christian, something Dad would hate. Dad got all the good parts anyway, gave the ring to a friend, the property to the young widow. What was a sixteen-year-old supposed to do – cry?

Widow one knew it was going to happen all along. She'd told widow two, hadn't bothered with three. You can't tell kids anything.

Everyone else rose up like a sigh at the end of a poorly edited film. Some of the tricks had failed, some had worked.

They all went home. That night they checked the closets. But he came in their dreams. When the doors flung open and windows popped out like a nuclear wish, the house was his. Because they gave it to him. What do you expect when you become friends with death? There was always one room he came to and did his routine—the parts exploded, the slow torture of his voice. Wasn't it enough they were sorry, they asked each other, knowing that once you invite the killer home, a person you meet while traveling, someone with credentials, he knows where you live.

He's at the control panel when you close your eyes. He just wants you to see what it's like. Mr. Green, Colonel Mustard, Miss Scarlet, in the dining room with the knife, the candle-stick, the revolver. Wiping red across his face like lipstick. The howl bagged and sold like a relic. The tips of his fingers cut off to avoid further identification. The only detail inadvertently right.

Each Time We Meet

IT'S LIKE DRIVING into the hot damp mouth of a dog, when the lawyer sister and I walk out of the airport terminal in South Carolina. At the ranch Father says, "It's no laughing matter. She keeps locking me out of the house. Says I killed your sister, but you know I haven't stepped foot out of here in months." His face is a puzzle of feelings.

"I told you not to come." Mother gestures with the tin box of candy. "I don't want you here, you understand? I don't want to see you." She gets up and walks past us into the kitchen, which opens into the living and dining areas in one of those floor plans that takes the secrets out of your life. We put our bags down. We haven't expected this. Although we knew she wouldn't like it, we aren't ready for the directness.

"There's no reason for you to be here. I didn't invite you." She slams the tin box down on the inlaid-tile counter, shades of brown and tan as always. "I'm not cooking, there's not enough food for you here. Don't expect anything. I didn't invite you." Although it is still early evening, she is dressed in a long nylon gown, stains of coffee marching up it as determined as mice. When she shakes her head and lights another cigarette, her eyes spark unnaturally, and her hair, which hasn't been combed in days, stands up around her face in a

halo of orange clumps thick as snakes. She hasn't been keeping the color, I notice.

"Hide the knives," the doctor sister urges long distance.
"She could get more violent." She hasn't been able to come.
Now she can be the voice of authority, the rest of us just the
incidence of her voice in action. "You know I'd be there if I
could. Just be careful." She calls the hospital and gets refer-
ences for rural South Carolina care.

Mother picks up the phone while I'm talking, yells, "How
dare you tell them that." The floor plan of the house is not arranged for such events. We're too close to each other, even
locked in the bedroom. Her hearing has become preter-
naturally powerful—the unhinging of the phone from its
cradle, the *click-click* as the dial rounds its route. We barely
start a conversation before she is on us.

At three o'clock in the morning, the door to our room
smashes into the bed we have shoved against it, like a bomb
in the hallway. Her body is lethal, and we push back with all
our might. The frogs have not silenced the southern night.
July breathes hot and insistent into the room, and the fan
pushes air away from itself in the dainty motion of a lady
waving a hand in front of her face.

At that moment I believe that the only person who could
make her behave is her ninety-nine-year-old mother, blind
and bedridden in southern Missouri. Her sharp Methodist
words could still straighten her daughter.

I spend the night dreaming of sieges. When I wake up, I
search all the drawers and closet shelves for photos. I clean
the house of myself, as best I can. I take my smiling baby and
hide it carefully in my purse where she can't get at it.

"He's an evil man. He killed her," she warns. "You know
that. I just want to get away." I want to let her, but this has
gone on too long. Maybe she has to be punished too.

"Don't believe anything she says," the doctor sister warns.
"Check her medication. Has she been taking her pills?"

Father shows me the dogwoods he planted for the dead sisters, mother's and then mine. The trees are both dead now because Mother left them in her hot southern car trunk while she played bridge all afternoon. "They were dead when she brought them home, but I planted them anyway." He is wheezing beside the fence around the house, needed to keep the animals out. Not snakes. It doesn't work for them.

"She won't let me tell our friends that your sister died." I own her, in death, I see. The insects' raw hum seems to turn the heat up. We go back inside, the sound scraping the inside of my ears, scouring. Father spreads his hands helplessly. "I keep watering them anyway." Later he leans across the kitchen table. "Did you see the body?"

She watches one television preacher after another—all morning, the healings, prayers, and pleas for money. Her gown grows dingier as she paces, sitting only to eat more candy from the almost empty ten-pound tin, smoke cigarettes, and drain another cup of the coffee she is brewing constantly, like some mad version of a good wife. She keeps the television turned up so loud that it is impossible to speak without shouting.

The youngest sister, the lawyer, argues with her, threatens to cry. Mother wisely ignores her, stopping only to pour an acid remark here or there. But by noon it is arranged. "Wish I could be there." The doctor sister has convinced a hospital forty-five minutes away to take her.

I know we're in for it when Mother chooses the black and yellow outfit for her ride to the mental hospital. It's her traveling costume. She doesn't go along easily. We threaten her, and the collective will wins out, although Father, the joker, tries to back down at the last minute. "Maybe she's not as bad as I thought." I shove him aside and open the door to the back seat for her. He sits in front because she won't let him in back.

In the car she begins to despair. Refuses to touch the dog. Talks about the Gestapo search of her house, her purse, her friends. She is on her way to the camps, on the move again. She opens her fears like a suitcase and begins unpacking. Father taunts her. I silently urge her on. Lawyer drives the boat-big Continental down the interstate, empty except for the occasional family returning from church. I notice that everyone else on the road looks normal. We must look normal too. Except for the rag of feeling we tie to the antenna that we keep raising and lowering electronically like a signal of distress at sea. The air conditioning can barely keep up with the heat, and she opens a window to let out the cigarette smoke.

"Do you have any money?" he asks her.

"You can't have it," she replies.

"Do you want more?" he asks.

"No, just put me in the welfare ward. Tell them that I don't have anything anymore." She unwraps a mint she has pulled from her purse. "I wore the wrong thing. Too bright. Yellow and black are too strident." She is on the verge of tears, and for the first time I want to reach out and touch her hand, but I don't.

"And tell them I didn't choose the colors in the house. They'll ask about that. Tell them I didn't buy those paintings. People gave them to me. They're not mine. They'll check on that—they always do. But I don't know—I don't know what colors are good. Something quiet. Not loud. I always choose the wrong colors."

We're silent in the car, which holds the speed limit and floats above the road, registering nothing of bumps and tiny waves in the new concrete.

We're all pretty drowned by the time we reach the hospital, despite the car's air conditioning.

"Do you know your daughter's dead?" They ask her at the hospital.

"Of course." Her mouth snaps shut like a purse. Lies—I send the look to the young doctor with a southern accent and a sympathy for my father.

It's tough convincing them to keep her for a few days, but it's a hundred and five degrees, and father's too old to stand out on that shadeless cement walk pleading to get into the house all day.

As we wait for the processing, she says to me, "This is goodbye. I never want to see you again."

"That's fine, Mother."

"I mean it. This is the last time I ever want to see you."

"I know," I tell her. "Every time I see you, I say goodbye for good."

We have finally reached an understanding. She is done with me. My older sister died, I am living. She won't see either of us.

We leave her sitting in the chrome and orange vinyl chairs of the modern patient lounge, marooned in her angry colors, her purse planted firmly on her lap, her knees together. Southern Methodist womanhood in the midst of everything she disapproves of: a cop show banging away on the large television, teenaged patients flopped in other chairs or pacing and arguing, snapping gum. The cajoling voice of the black social worker is the final sign of family injustice. "Rose, you want to come with me? Rose, may I call you Rose?"

"No," my mother replies, in her angry-bee dress, "you may call me Mrs. Taylor." She plants her purse more firmly on her lap and tightens her knees, pretending not to notice us walking through the double glass doors into the late afternoon humidity.

What in the World

THE MISSIONARY stood on the corner of Fourth and Wabasha, uncertain which way to go. The doctor had told him four to six miles a day. He always tried to do what another professional told him. At first he had tried to take the dog with him, but he grew tired of the constant drag on the leash after a few blocks. The dog, after all, hadn't been ordered to walk four to six miles or lose his legs to diabetes.

It was always something, the missionary thought, as he stood on the street corner in downtown St. Paul. Always something. First his father, then the Lord. Now this. Oh sure, there had been things in between—his wife this spring. The police detective across the street who drank and had plowed into his front porch one day. Broad daylight. After that the city had forced the detective into early retirement. Not like the missionary, who had had to beg to be let off the hook finally. It was a first case, really, for his tiny church, the People of the Cross. You died in the field. It was expected of you if you took the call. You didn't pay into Social Security, and you weren't expected to show up at home years later asking for your retirement fund.

He and his wife had both become sick. They wanted to be back among their own kind. Hard-working white people. It was a miracle the day they found the house in this old Czech neighborhood. No shaded faces to look at. No strange cooking odors. No music that twanged discordant on his nerves, fine as hair. It was all the way he'd remembered it.

His wife had sown flowers and vegetables like a hedge around the white stucco bungalow. When she had died in the spring, he'd continued with her efforts although his heart wasn't in it. He had faith that the tomatoes would ripen and bear at the right time. If they didn't, he vowed, he'd plow them under and plant grass instead.

He glanced up and down the intersection. It pleased him, the smell and noise of cars on a hot summer day. At night, lying in bed, he hummed to the rumble and clatter of the trains going by two blocks away. "Like music," he'd told his wife. "It's like music. Thank God we came back." His wife's reply was a spasm of planting or washing. She never tired of running the clothes washer and dryer, the only things she'd asked for when they retired. He bought her the dishwasher as a surprise for her and was himself surprised when she slid down the wall, her face in her hands, bawling.

It was unlike her to have fits of emotion. Still, as he recalled the scene now, on the corner of Fourth and Wabasha, she had been more emotional before the call had come and they'd packed themselves off to missionary life in the field. Almost as if she'd left that part of herself in storage in the boxes of personal items the church had permitted them to store in the basement. Many years later when they returned, most of those things were rotted or mildewed beyond use. They'd left the boxes in disgust. Let the church clean up the mess. If it ever got around to it. Things were hopping these days with the church: new members and more enthusiasm than the early days when he left his family house, not following his father before him into the brewery but marrying the girl he'd met at church and then going into the field.

When his legs started to ache from the heat and standing, he knew he'd have to make a choice. To go down Wabasha meant risking the onslaught from the stores, the clothes for men of an age he'd missed, the furniture, the gadgets he still had no use for. Either way, this was the part of the walk he didn't like.

The missionary stood on the corner for a few more minutes, studying the possibilities and watching people as they hurried through their afternoon, moving against the heat at a pace that rocked the air into waves away from themselves. In the field he'd had to accommodate himself to the rhythms of the tropical weather. At first he hadn't minded. He was on his honeymoon. His young wife was loving, giving. After that it was cycles of rice planting, growing, harvesting, the wet season, the mud, the insects, the rot that invaded his fingers and toes. All that required that he move slowly, deliberately, like a man asleep. For forty years he'd slept. Then one day he'd awakened, walked into the tiny house that clung like a leech to the side of the little church he'd built in a clearing, and told his wife to pack her things. They were going home, they were retiring.

He'd just come back from the international field hospital six miles away. They'd told him it was diabetes. Now that they were both sick, his wife with heart problems and him with diabetes, they could go home, he figured. So he'd wired the church in St. Paul, sold almost everything they owned, refusing to let his wife keep most of the native pieces she'd collected, packed the suitcases they'd brought forty years before, and boarded the first plane home.

His wife hadn't spoken a word to him until a week later when he found the house and they moved in with furniture donated by the church. He was the first to come home from the field, they told him, but they weren't going to let him go hungry and unhoused.

Anyway, they had more money now. He knew they figured the old couple wouldn't last long. He intended to fool them. He'd get the most out of his retirement. They'd be paying twenty years from now, he vowed. His wife hadn't had the same determination: she'd dropped pretty fast. One year at home and she was dead, fallen in the yard with the trowel in her hand, a smudge of dirt like a bruise on her calf. He'd always see that, he thought, as he walked slowly down Fourth Street. That bruise of dirt. As if it was supposed to tell him something. As if she had wanted it to tell him something. But he couldn't understand it. He shook his head and almost ran into someone coming the other way. Putting up both hands as if in benediction, he stepped sideways. He'd gotten into the habit of looking down as he walked, and he looked up only with conscious effort. Sometimes it was hard to square the shoulders and hold that twenty-pound weight of head on a neck that seemed so tired.

Besides, the missionary realized as he looked around him, maybe he didn't want to see where he was going. In a few blocks the tall buildings would drop back, bowing out like gentlemen, leaving him to confront the housing project. He liked the way downtown seemed guarded by the stone and steel office buildings that blocked any attempt to move the human disarray of the housing project in on it. Sure, they could walk the streets, but the buildings locked arms and resisted the dirt and living they attempted.

Soon he came to the block just before the two-block section that housed several hundred Hmong refugees. He stopped. Today with the heat and humidity he didn't think he could run the gauntlet of smells and sounds: the weaving around the tiny children masquerading as Americans in shorts and tennis shoes on tricycles, the unblinking stares of the old women in long colorful skirts and embroidered blouses who watched him from their doorsteps, the smart-aleck snickers of the teenaged boys who had already learned to wear tight jeans and T-shirts while they drove around in fast new cars. He couldn't afford a car—how could they?

Glancing around one last time before continuing, he noticed a small street to the right that he must have missed on other days. He set off more briskly than before. This street would take him closer to West Seventh, Old Fort Road now, where he always ended his walk, two miles down to the brewery for a free drink of spring water, then back home to Michigan Street.

He remembered as a small boy going to the brewery with his father. Staring at the huge vats and powerful machines stamping caps and labels on the battalions of long-necked brown bottles that marched along tiny rollers on a route around half the main floor, like a train going through the mountains, the cars swaying back and forth, glistening in the light. Later in the field, when he'd taken trains from one place to another, they'd proven a disappointment, crowded and smelly and bumpy, enough to jar your bones out of place.

If he'd been looking up, he would have noticed that the way he chose was leading him into an even poorer section of town than the one he was avoiding. The houses stood with siding molting down, gutters broken and rusted, and screen doors with holes the size of children and small animals. Some of the doors even flopped on one hinge, as if a wind could take them down like broken tree limbs. Along the street, battered rusting cars sat waiting.

When the missionary put his foot on the shards of a whiskey bottle broken on the sidewalk, he jerked his head up as if the tinkle of glass had come from above. A few steps away stood a huge Indian, leaning against a streetlight, his arms crossed and his head down as if in deep concentration. The missionary wasn't afraid. When he was almost on top of him, the man raised his head and unfolded his arms. In his left hand he clutched a paving brick. The missionary recognized it from the ones his father had taken when their street had been ripped up for trolley tracks. They'd made a little brick patio out back of their house. He remembered how difficult it was to shovel the snow from the bricks the way his father liked it. Always so much shoveling of snow. He had thought about that a lot in the field, where there was no snow at all, and after many years had almost come to miss it, when it was too hot to sleep. But right now he should be paying attention to the Indian blocking his path.

While the missionary searched for the appropriate smile and greeting, to let the Indian know he was a man of the cloth, the Indian came a half step closer. Suddenly the old man felt his heart take a huge surge and knock, as if the assembly line had faltered and the bottles were swaying, threatening to topple. The old man put out his hand to steady himself.

He felt himself going down, his knees letting go, folding their hinges, and then he felt hands grabbing him under the arms, laying him down like a good suit of clothes on the bed. Straightening him out. The hands patted him softly on the head, then the cheeks.

The missionary felt he would be sick in a minute from the smell that spread over him like a sheet. He couldn't catch his breath, so he had to keep tugging the noxious air into his lungs. Then something else tugged at him, and he rolled his head to the other side and opened his eyes. The houses swam like fish in a circle around him, and overhead, towering behind them like a visiting god, the Schmidt Brewery sign winked on and off in red neon against the perfect blue afternoon sky.

The missionary closed his eyes, remembering how cool the paving bricks felt that summer he built the patio with his father and brothers—cool, like the dirt under the thicket of lilacs on the north of the house where the dog used to hide. He took a deep breath, pulling in all the smells of earth and rotting blossoms and heat.

"That's right. Keep breathing."

The missionary could feel the shaking fingers undoing his shirt buttons and the surprising cool rush of air that welcomed his skin.

When a Dream

SARAH HAD PARKED carelessly the night before, too exhausted from the drive to worry about other cars or people.
When she woke up, she noticed that she was probably going to have to move if anyone else wanted to come up the old
road to the top. She was blocking the turnaround in the
clearing. At first she thought maybe she should get out,
unpack the camping equipment, and pitch her tent, but
looking around, she decided against it. She could just as
easily sleep in the car, the family station wagon. She'd worried about taking the car they did the grocery shopping and
running around in, but she'd decided that Johann could use
the company car for that. The kids wouldn't care, and she
needed the station wagon to climb over these back moun-
tain roads. In the note she'd explained it all. Now, glancing
around her, she was happy she'd brought its sturdiness to
comfort her. The woods here weren't lovely, dark, and
deep, as Robert Frost would have said. This wasn't New
England, though, but Washington state, and around her
spread the rock outcrops and thin soil of the mountainous
region she'd chosen. Sarah knew she was right in her cal-
culations. There wasn't any question about it: it would start
here. She'd wait for them.

She'd brought two weeks' worth of food and supplies, figuring that'd be enough so she could spend some time with them before she went back home. Finally, finally, the waiting was going to be over. She'd decided to keep a journal about her experiences, to share with Johann and the children when she got back or to publish for a wider audience once it was discovered that she had met them. She was a scholar. She wasn't embarrassed by the notion of recording her perceptions for others to read. She'd been trained to value her insights that way. And she was way ahead of the game. She'd figured it all out, so she was prepared.

It wasn't until the third day that Sarah was interrupted. She'd gotten along fine, eating from her little supply of food, writing and reading, taking walks to stretch her legs in the pleasant woods in late September. Very nice. She wished she'd brought along Euell Gibbons's books so she could identify some edible plants. Might as well, if you have time, and that might help the visitors when they came. But the truth of the matter was that she hoped they had all that information at their fingertips. She hoped so because there were some areas she wasn't certain enough about to report on. She didn't want to appear ignorant in front of them. She had a doctorate from the University of Minnesota. And she had been a sister in the Order of Holy Angels. Well, maybe she'd better leave that part out. After all, she'd left the order. She didn't want to tell them that. It might make her look as though she couldn't be trusted—a quitter or something—when in truth she was prepared to wait forever for them to arrive, although she knew they'd be there within two weeks. That's what she'd written on the note to Johann. Two, maybe three weeks. Then she'd come home and tell them all about it. She hadn't told him where she was going. No point in alarming him. He might worry about her going all the way to Washington state.

But in the early afternoon on the third day she heard a car engine struggling up the road, and in a minute it burst into the clearing behind her: a mottled green Chevy station wagon, years older than hers. Behind the wheel a small middle-aged man sat humped and squinting like a frog in the middle of a dry pond. The car continued to cough and choke, the smoke filling the clearing, but the man sat there as if he'd never seen another car in his life. She opened the door, got out, hesitated, then walked to his door. She was surprised to see the window rolled up in the heat of early afternoon, and she gestured for him to unroll it. He did, reluctantly, squinting at her.

"Turn it off," she told him. His hand leaped to the key and obeyed.

"Why, lady, I thought you was them. I did. I thought I was too late. Why, I admit it took me by surprise that they'd be smart enough to make the ship look like a Buick station wagon. But then, they could, sure, you know—they're smart."

Sarah struggled for a moment, unable to decide what to say or how she felt. She wanted to say, "Well, how did *you* know?" But she didn't want to insult him. She wanted to tell him to leave, but she knew he had a right to stay. He already knew what was going to happen in that clearing. She decided to welcome him because finally it was relief she felt. Although she hadn't admitted it to herself and certainly not to Johann in the note, she was a tiny bit worried that she might be wrong. Now with the appearance of this pickle farmer or whatever he was, she knew she was correct.

"Surprised, ain't ya?" When he grinned, his crooked, mossy teeth seemed to hang out over his lower jaw like a precipice the rest of his face might fall off of. When he stopped, the teeth disappeared behind his lips. "Gotcha, didn't I? It's my plate. First ones got knocked out in a bar. Next ones got broke when the dang car here dropped on me while I was repairing it. But I took some glue and set them in again. Trouble was, I jiggled them a mite before they set, and now I can't get them straight again. Crazy glue. You know that guy gets his hat stuck on that steel beam, and it carries him up about twenty feet? Now I slide the teeth in and out— just a little joke when I meet people."

When he noticed that she wasn't even trying to smile, he added, "Don't worry, ma'am. I don't do it more than once. See?" He grinned again, pulling his lips up like a big snake reared back on its tail. It made her uncomfortable, so she nodded and waved a hand to let him know it was all right.

"So you're here for them too? How did you know?" she asked. He took a screwdriver from the seat beside him, inserted it into the hole in the door where the handle should have been, and gave it a quick shove with his shoulder. She stepped back just as the door came flying open with a high metallic squeal. He kept himself from falling out after it by grabbing the steering wheel.

"Well, missy," he said climbing out gingerly, as if he wasn't certain that his skinny little legs would hold him up. "I read a lot. And I keep myself a little notebook." He was hopping back and forth beside the car to limber up, looking like a rooster on parade in front of a bunch of hens, she thought, with his elbows flapping at his sides as though he'd start crowing any minute.

"But—" she started. He interrupted her. Reaching into his back pocket he pulled out a nineteen-cent spiral notebook, the brown cover worn down to mottled vanilla from the constant rubbing in his pocket.

He grinned at her. "I got it all here. Like a message from God—that's what it was. I knew it the first thing—a message from God."

When she reached out for it, he pulled it back and pushed it into the pocket of his dirty jeans, shaking his head. "No sirree, no ma'am. No one sees this. Not even the wife. I told her, 'Don't you ever touch it. If I leave it in my pants, you don't wash those pants, not till I get there and pull it out. But don't you touch it.' I kept my word. I never let nobody touch it, and because of that I'm here. I *was* going to be the first." He looked at her as if he'd just realized something. "How'd *you* find out?" She felt like an insect, the way he stood there licking his long tongue around his thin lips and squinting and blinking at her.

"I read about it too. I went all the way back to the third century for some of my information." She tried to find some common ground for them.

"Ha," he belched a short laugh. "Why'd you go to all that trouble? Those old books cost a fortune."

She nodded. "So how did you discover it?"

"Comic books, mostly Marvel and DC, and the movies." Then he laughed hard, only it didn't sound like a laugh. It gurgled and sucked like something thick cooking on the stove. "Lady, that's pretty funny, ain't it?" He gasped in between his choking sobs of laughter.

It had already snowed twice, but each time it melted again immediately afterward. They were down to a box of Cocoa Puffs he'd brought and some stale crackers she'd thrown in as an afterthought five weeks before, when she'd left her family. They'd moved into her car after two weeks, for warmth at night, in their sleeping bags pressed against each other. It had taken Sarah a while to accept Orrin, but the excitement they shared over their discovery and the reassurance the other person provided gradually wore down her resistance. Besides, he was very discreet about keeping his teeth in his mouth.

Although they'd had some water when they came and collected when it rained or snowed, they'd still been on strict rations for over a week now. Sarah didn't care. She didn't feel much like eating or drinking anymore. Lately, she noticed, she was very tired. She seemed to wake up in the morning only when Orrin shook her shoulder hard enough to rattle the whole car, and she fell asleep almost immediately after her half cup of Cocoa Puffs. For lunch he'd wake her with a sip of water and half a cracker, but she couldn't stomach that, anyway. And dinner was more Cocoa Puffs.

Looking up at Orrin's worried face, drawn even thinner by their fasting, she laughed to realize that regardless of size he somehow continued to resemble a frog.

"Missy, you got to eat something. I'm going to drive us out of here if you don't try to eat some of these."

When she only shook her head, he pretended he was trying to feed a child. "Now watch Poppa, watch Orrin. See, ummmm, good. Now you try. Open wide. That's a girl. Now chew. No, no, don't let them dribble out that way. Chew, darn it."

"I'm okay," she whispered to him a few days later when his ear was close to her mouth. "I'm okay. I just don't want to miss them, Orrin. You can't drive us out. We'll miss them. It's the best thing that ever happened. You know that, so don't leave. Orrin, don't leave. We have to have faith. We have to wait for them."

Whispering was better in the woods, she decided. That way, their voices wouldn't carry, and the visitors wouldn't think they were a loud, boisterous people. She practiced now, as she lay perfectly still in the back of the station wagon, the quiet, the immobility she had learned in the novitiate, waiting for Christ. She remembered sprawling on the floor at the foot of his cross for hours in her little room, learning to forget the winter cold as she concentrated on the heat of pain spreading through his body and then hers. Once she was certain she heard him whispering to her, "Wait for me, Sarah. Wait for me." She responded like a deer to noise, leaping up and almost running out of the room, frantic that her prayers had been heard.

When she told her spiritual guide, Sister Mary Vesco, Mary smiled, patted her hand, and put her to work in the kitchen for the next three months. "Too much time spent alone, my dear. Not good for you to be alone so much. Come work here beside these poor souls who must toil daily for their bread."

She'd known it was punishment for having heard Christ speak. He never spoke again, she noticed. Although she tried to regain her former concentration at the foot of the cross, she had grown too impatient. After long hours on her feet, side by side with the dim-witted boy who washed dishes and the equally dim-witted girl who helped the cook, she was too tired.

Later, when the dim-witted girl was blamed for the new-born baby found stuffed in the toilet on the second floor, Sarah wondered that she had never noticed a pregnancy and that she could barely imagine the pain the girl must have endured giving birth alone, silent, in the upstairs bathroom. And the horror as the infant began to squall, followed by the silencing: handfuls of toilet paper stuffed in its mouth. Then it was dropped, breathing still, into the bowl, and it was breathing still when Sister Frederick went to the stall and almost fainted, first imagining, as she later told them repeatedly, that it had come up through the sewer pipes, some huge water rat, before she realized it was a live child.

They said the dim-witted girl from the kitchen was the mother, because the child bore a resemblance. It was dim-witted, too. Sarah had often wondered if they'd made a mistake, remembering the bewildered head shaking no, as she was led away after the bundle of new baby was refused. The child was placed in a home, as all dim-witted children should be, Sister Frederick assured everyone—a good Catholic home where they would teach it better than to have relations with men and stuff babies in toilets.

Now as Sarah lay in the back of the car, hands alternately folded across her chest or down at her sides like a medieval pope in a stone sepulcher, she regained her former powers of concentration. Her body began to cooperate again, the dull aching muscles and organs transferring themselves into pinpoints of sensation that carried one clear message on a continuous route into her consciousness: "Wait for me, Sarah. Wait for me."

And somehow in her dreamy joy, the figure of Christ crawled off the cross, stood whole and manly again, not the squirmy, battered self she had given up on but rather a man, larger than life, dressed in a silver space suit with his helmet under his arm glowing like a jeweled crown, and behind him ten more, all tall and strong, powerful travelers through the misery of dark sky and dead stars, and she was there to greet them.

Finally, like a ghostly lover, they came in one motion to her, pulled her to her feet, and outfitted her with a space suit that seemed to fit like her own skin, custom-made. Oh, they had known then, known that she was waiting, had prepared for her. As she stood there, the leader bent to her his face, bright and clear and pure. He seemed to be trying to say something to her. Although she couldn't understand what it was, he kept pointing to her ear. As she turned her head slightly so he could speak into it, she noticed the label on the back of his space suit: "Made in Taiwan, 80% polyester, 20% cotton, machine washable."

"Ooh," she wailed, and a rough hand shook her hard and slapped her face. She could feel that.

"Missy, wake up. Open your eyes." When she did, Orrin was hovering over her like a small, ugly guardian angel. "What's the matter? What's the matter with you?"

"Oh, Orrin, machine-washable spacesuits made in Taiwan. Orrin, don't you see?"

Orrin sat back on his heels, head and shoulders hunched

over by the roof of the station wagon. When he shook his head and let out his breath, she noticed how white it was, a little puff of smoke, but he didn't smoke. She turned her head and saw that it had snowed again. When she looked back at him, she noticed he was shivering.

"Orrin, you have to get into your bag. It's too cold out there. Come on." She whispered as loudly as she could, but he shook his head.

She nodded, and he shook his head again. "No, ma'am, if you don't have any more faith than that, why, I'm going to have to sit out here and wait by myself. You might as well get up and drive back home, after all the waiting you done, and now this."

"But, Orrin." She wanted to laugh, but her body was too weak. She could feel the laugh down there, tickling her as it coughed around in her ribs. "I just had a dream. I didn't mean anything."

"Blaspheme those fellers up there, they'll skip right over us. Land somewhere else. Another planet. You'll have it on your shoulders, lady." Orrin was feeling self-righteous, as he always did when they discussed spacemen, especially the religion of the spacemen. "They'll be Christians," he had told her. "God wouldn't let no other kind come here. This is a Christian world." When she'd tried to argue, he'd only gotten more adamant: "And they'll probably be Baptist, too." Then he'd wrapped his arms around himself tightly and rocked back and forth, nodding and blinking his eyes real hard, as if he was seeing something happen that he was almost too excited to watch. "Probably be Baptist."

Sarah couldn't make him understand that most of the world wasn't even Christian and that only a tiny part of the Christian part was Baptist. "Don't you try to Jew me down with facts," he'd warned her, and she'd given up. She'd never told him she had been a nun or even a Catholic.

"Forgive me, Orrin," she whispered later and tried to smile, although she could barely feel the muscles of her face anymore, she'd been working so hard at concentrating on waiting. He sat rigid for a minute more, watching her. Then he nodded once and crawled over to the other bag, got in, and lay down. Pulling her head over to his chest, he began to stroke her dirty blond hair, which hung in thick greasy strands, smoothing and tucking it as if he was making a bed. Sarah could hear the low hum of his heart through the bag, and closing her eyes, she let the music sail her off to sleep.

A while later Orrin addressed the back of her head. "It's all right, missy. You didn't hurt my feelings none. It's all right." He paused, then offered, "They'll be here soon now, real soon, Missy Sarah."

Just Your Friend

AT FIRST it was only mildly odd. After a month on the job, clippings began to appear under her door—either yellowing *Life* articles about famous American writers obviously pulled from files kept from the heyday of the publication or cartoons neatly scissored from current *New Yorker*s. It was the latter that gave Sister Aspira away. She was wildly addicted to *The New Yorker*.

Mary Masters didn't know what to do with all the paper. She filed the first couple of contributions under "twentieth-century American," but only after waiting a month to see if the person who sent them would come forward. Or to be sure that she wasn't supposed to pass them along, on the hand-delivered route the English department believed important to their communication. With only five of them, Mary wondered if they couldn't just meet in the hallway or something, but she was new, so she tried to respect the rules. When no one claimed the clipping on William Faulkner's house, she reluctantly put it away, feeling somehow wrong about it, as if she had been shoplifting or had found a ten dollar bill—something in her possession that was clearly not hers.

This wrongness became the sad shadow under her door each morning. She cringed as she noticed the blocked light when she walked down the hall toward her office. Not only that, she was arriving later than eight o'clock, the time that the sisters seemed to prescribe as the appropriate one – they mostly had eight o'clock classes – a wrongness in itself, since after her first year of college teaching she had timidly questioned the urgency of her teaching a class when she was so asleep. It had been her first step toward having a voice and had cost her weeks of tossing and turning at night while her husband's breathing sounded like a car with a backfire, dirty spark plugs – pop, sputter.

Her request was granted immediately, with no comment. She knew the wrongness of it when the schedule was printed and only her name appeared without an early class. To balance, she'd offered to teach the night course the college was experimenting with – commuter, adult, after-work types enrolling instead of sticking to family life, yard work. They all wanted to be writers. It frightened her sometimes – all those words and faces that might appear under her door someday, after they'd aged decently in Sister Aspira's files.

The cartoons from *The New Yorker* were another matter. Since they showed no ragged edges like the literary pieces, it was clear that they were to be taken more seriously. Perhaps, Mary decided, she should display them on her door the way Sister Aspira did: each morning a new cartoon, above which an arrow pointed. Like most *New Yorker* cartoons they were pretty funny. Never off-color. While the cartoons slipped under Mary's door were always literary or had to do with the writers she was teaching at night, the cartoons on Aspira's door were broad-ranging. That surprised Mary. Should she feel badly? She wasn't even sure about what. But maybe she should. So she tried circulating them in class. She hated sending the neat squares of *New Yorker* paper around the room.The obligatory grins and hee-haws for the spice of college life: literary cartoons. She felt like giving a pop quiz every time someone laughed.

By the second year Sister Aspira began to send her clips of inspiringly difficult quizzes from *The London Times* or *The Atlantic*. Since Mary could never supply the correct words or dates or the answers to the grammatical errors, she cringed every time she opened one of the folded pieces of paper, in a recycled envelope with someone else's name carefully scratched out. She was sure Aspira could do all the quizzes. She told her husband that. He said, "You're paranoid. Sounds like a nice lady." Then he dropped off to sleep.

While his untuned breathing ran her thoughts wildly into the middle of the night, she could feel Aspira slipping down the hall and passing through the door to her office as if she had a key. Maybe she did. Recently she'd taken to leaving the clippings right on her desk, like a reminder of the wrongness of the mass of paper and books clotting the surface. Somehow each new clipping glowed and rustled more brightly, so she immediately knew it was there when she entered the room.

Graduate school hadn't prepared Mary for this. She'd been a good student—thorough, sometimes even imaginative in her approach to literature. But she'd always tried to be careful. She'd avoided trouble: students who led noisy lives, switching lovers or spouses, haggling with teachers, parading with the undergraduates against the war. She'd met Ronald, her businessman husband, gotten married, and moved after her degree to this small town and small job in the Midwest, at a small college run by the Sisters of Hope. Everything on schedule. If she'd read about herself in a story, she could point out her problem. But why didn't anyone say anything? Why did she feel so wrong? Nothing she read seemed to fit exactly.

Her students didn't seem puzzled by life the way she was these days. They had conclusions, solutions. When a character's life got out of whack, they advised counseling, AA, vegetarianism. Don't drink pop with Nutrasweet, they warned her. Get off that sugar, or you'll be sorry. When a character had a real problem, they wrestled with it like television evangelists, talk-radio doctors. They weren't ashamed of their own confessions, which invariably followed. Although she tried to avoid personal connections, the students insisted on them. They even asked her how many husbands she'd had, as if they had a right to know.

But that was the problem: the wrongness of everything. And the crack under her door filled with reminders.

That wasn't all. After six years of Mary's service in the English department, coincidental with Mary's receiving tenure and agreeing with her husband that they had found themselves quite the little spot, Sister Aspira ceased the clipping service. Or at least she slackened off. It made Mary anxious to see the morning light spreading like melted margarine under her office door. Without the envelopes on the floor underneath or waiting on the desk, the room seemed unchecked, dangerous.

Often Mary opened the door with caution, as if her office had taken on strangers in her absence. Something always seemed amiss. When she did receive a clipping, it was from the *Sunday Times Magazine*. Newsprint disturbed her, especially if a color spread were included.

She must have done something really beyond the pale — that was all she could say to herself. At home Mary was short-tempered. At Christmas she broke several ornaments while unpacking the glass spheres from their tissue. They were part of the antique collection Mary and her husband had bought.

"What's wrong with you?" her husband asked, as he swept up shards of pale lemon and orange glass.

"Everything," Mary said, and she let another ball slip between her fingers. It bounced and smashed simultaneously with a sound like a gull cry.

"What are you doing?" her husband asked between gritted teeth, then stooped to brush some of the glass away from her. He wasn't sure she'd remember he was there beneath her.

"It's the box," she said, flapping her arms at her sides in despair. "I knew I shouldn't, but I did, and now she'll know." Mary reached for another ball.

"No, no, that's okay." Her husband guided her down off the chair and located her on the sofa, away from the ornaments. "Take a rest," he advised. "Now what were you saying?" For all her levelheadedness, he was beginning to feel twinges of worry. Maybe it wasn't normal to be so normal.

"It was her box. Don't you see?" She flopped her hands in her lap.

He nodded solemnly. It was Christmas—he'd have to be understanding. She was often odd this time of year, he'd noticed.

"I was just lazy, that's all. Now she'll see it in the hall, filled with my night students' writing portfolios."

"How can she tell it's hers? Just a cardboard box." He was making progress with the tree now that she was busy with Sister What's-her-name.

"She knows everything. I'm not even Catholic, and she knows me. If I sneeze in my office, she hands me Kleenex an hour later as she passes my door."

"Sounds considerate."

"You'll see." Sure enough, in March a sign appeared in the tiny faculty bathroom Mary shared with the sisters. Aspira had of late been storing her extra files and boxes in the corner between the step stool, which permitted the most diminutive nun a view of her teeth in the palm-size round mirror tacked beside the door, and the orange crate with a linen dresser scarf thrown over it, which served as the table for the cinnamon-scented bug spray, extra brown paper towels so harsh they rubbed the skin off her hands like an emery board, and industrial toilet paper that was thin enough to see through and that crackled like wrapping paper in her hands as she pulled it off the roll—she hated the idea of the tender nun bottoms coming in contact with that paper. Perched on the shelf above the sink were a big square plastic dispenser of hand lotion, the cheap kind from the discount drugstore, and a hair brush with a few strands of gray hair woven through its black bristles.

Last December all Sister Aspira's boxes had borne signs claiming them. But the one with FREE BOOKS!!! was almost empty. Mary needed a box outside her door for her students to drop off their portfolios of writing the next morning. It was nine-fifteen at night. She shouldn't have, but she dumped the free books into another box, which seemed to contain fourteenth-century literature. She probably wouldn't even notice, Mary thought on that cold, snowy last night of classes.

Now, in March, a sign appeared defending the remainder of the boxes: "To Mary and all other box stealers . . ."

Mary gasped as she read the sign, pulled up her panty hose, forgot to wash her hands, and rushed out of the bathroom without raising the handle on the toilet, as the sign, taped above the little porcelain gizmo, ordered in Sister Aspira's handwriting.

For a week Mary was sick with outrage and guilt. She composed clever literary replies. She'd Addison her Steele, Boswell her Johnson, Macbeth her Hamlet. She stopped making sense. She spent one sleepless night mentally collecting all the boxes in town, especially from liquor stores, and stacking them outside Aspira's door. A triumphant smile leered at her across the dawn-filled room. It was hers, and it was wrong.

She did nothing, except to consider going back home two mornings later, when she saw the familiar shape under the door as she hurried down the hall with her dark glasses on so Sister Aspira wouldn't notice her. The dark glasses helped until she neared the office. Then the block of shadow dividing the light made her moan and rip the glasses off. She hurried the unlocking—she thought she'd shake the door off its hinges. Inside, she slammed the door and looked around, half-expecting that she'd closed someone in rather than out.

At her feet the clipping throbbed like a small animal's heart.

Someone Else to Love

Day One

"DEAR ANYBODY, I'm sick of heart and mind, There is nothing to say to anyone anymore. You all know who you are. Betty Frid."

When Jeremiah got home from work, changed clothes, and came into the living room, he found the note taped to the television screen. The fifth that week. He put it on top of the television with the rest and turned on the tube. He thought of it as the tube: it fed him, he fed it. He never forgot to pay the electric bill, although the car payment was always overdue and the mortgage company sent threatening notes monthly. Once even a letter: "Who gave you the right . . ." He ignored it and sent the payment two weeks late as always. But the words stuck with him—who, indeed.

The screen brightened, spreading gray white from the center outward, like a nuclear bomb test, then cooled to an even tone as figures emerged from the fog of light. It took another thirty seconds for the whole thing to snap into focus and the sound to rise up like an Easter Sunday choir, low, then loud and distinct. On the other set, the color would've snapped in by now too, Jeremiah remembered regretfully. It had always seemed like a reward for his hard work when it came on, with that little snap as if someone inside the tube had clicked his fingers.

But Floyd, Betty's brother, had repossessed that one. Floyd had loaned it to them to use for two weeks while he went on vacation once, and they'd kept it a year and a half before Floyd finally came to get it. Something about having the television stashed in the corner of the living room, like hiding a fugitive from justice, had made Jeremiah appreciate the gesture of full living color more than usual. He could hardly wait to get home to watch the tube that year and a half. He even stopped going out with the few friends they had so he could watch television. Who knew when Floyd would reappear on the front porch waving a warrant for the color television. Jeremiah'd already made up his mind that he wouldn't let Floyd in, though Floyd had been there several times during the television's sabbatical and had always nodded at it, as if they were acquaintances on the street. "Still working," he'd say, half to Jeremiah and half to the television.

Then one Saturday afternoon, out of the blue, Betty had gotten off the phone and come in to where Jeremiah was watching the high-diving competition on *Wide World of Sports*. One man had already almost drowned, been pulled out by the efficient rescue team, strapped onto a flat board in case his neck was broken, and hustled off in an ambulance, when Betty announced, "Floyd's coming over to get the TV now," and left the room.

Well, that had ruined the diving competition for Jeremiah. He did manage to hear the commentator say that the diver was okay, that he'd just been knocked out. Jeremiah felt mixed relief and regret. It might have been more amazing to watch death, unplanned that way in the middle of an organized event, something they couldn't edit away, like bad audience response, and dub in later.

Finally, with his concentration broken, Jeremiah had turned off the television and had gone to the basement, then the attic and garage to look for the old black-and-white. When he couldn't find it anywhere, he came back into the house, calling for Betty.

"Sold it" was all she'd say as she peeled the potatoes, making neat curls, which dropped delicate as snowflakes onto the little pile in the sink. She'd paused and looked up at him, a long look that Jeremiah couldn't understand. "Floyd's bringing his old black-and-white cabinet for you."

He'd nodded and left the room. The image of the potatoes, raw and white as larvae, with the eyes cut out, stacking up beside the sink, stayed with him as he sat down to wait for Floyd in the living room, with the color television turned off.

"Betty, Betty, Betty," he said to himself over and over again as he fetched supper from the kitchen. When Jeremiah had left the priesthood, he'd wanted to find a woman as plain as margarine. He had. Betty was working in the office where he found a job. She was a file clerk with no chance of advancement because of her typing. It took her too long to correct all her mistakes under pressure, but she was very fast and efficient with the files. And her memory was perfect. She hadn't lost or misplaced anything in over eight years, they told him. That was Betty. She never got sick or missed work from partying too long on a weekend or because she'd really rather be somewhere else. That was what had drawn Jeremiah to Betty in the first place. She was never straining to get away, like a dog frantic on a leash, as Jeremiah had felt once or twice.

No, that wasn't true for him either. Some of the other men who'd left had been like that—young, bright stars who felt the confinement of the priesthood, in the strange new world of the seventies, etch their souls like acid. Jeremiah hadn't felt like that. If anything, he'd been worn smooth and dull as a table knife by the routine and the comfort the priesthood afforded him. Sometimes he thought he'd left because he was jostled out of place by all the turmoil going on around him, as if he was a nut or bolt in a gearbox that started to fly apart going down the highway, taking all the pieces with it as it exploded, sending him bouncing and rolling away into the grass. One day he was typing forms and letters as always, adding figures on the calculator along with the tape because he always double-checked, and the next day he was out. Jeremiah knew there were steps in between, but when he tried to repeat them, they wouldn't hold. As if the vertical was out, it was a slow blurring roll of figures and voices that lost their distinction in his memory.

Someone had given him the name of the Pinnacle Insurance Company, which he now worked for in St. Paul, told him they were Catholic and would hire him. He didn't care about their religious preference, but he had gone and taken the job anyway. Clerk-typist. He was the only man among a squad of women who typed and gossiped and competed around him. It had taken him a good half year to spot Betty among the other women who worked there, because she was so plain. He knew enough to realize that a fancy woman could cause trouble. The other priests had told stories at dinner every night about the trouble men had with women in the world. Although he didn't do much in that line—his office skills were too much in demand—his occasional excursions into the confessional led him to the basic information that you had less trouble with a plain woman.

Besides, he was plain. Some of the women thought he'd chosen Betty because he was shy, uncomfortable with women. He occasionally overheard them discussing him among their other topics. They acted as if he were deaf, the way adults talk in front of children. But in fact he wasn't uncomfortable in the job or with women. That had never been a problem for Jeremiah. He amazed the other priests and ex-priests because his transition was so easy.

His counselor—they were all assigned one in that period of adjustment—simply folded his hands and talked about fishing up north when Jeremiah came in. He was paid by the church for six months of counseling, no matter what. "You could be anything, Jerry. You know that? You're just the sort of person we need more of. Too many people get so wound up about things. Like my son. When we go fishing, he has to have this certain kind of bait, this particular kind of line and jig and so on. He's never comfortable unless the boat sits just so. It drives me nuts. We spend half our time fiddling with things, trying to get them right so he can sit down and shut up. Then the fish are gone by the time he's finally ready. Drives me nuts." The counselor usually paused in a discussion like this and flashed him a wise look. "That kind of person drive *you* nuts, Jerry?"

Jeremiah knew he was supposed to say yes, but in truth he couldn't, so he just shook his head. He was interested in the counselor's stories, though, and felt a twinge of sadness the day the man stood up, shook his hand, and told him their sessions were over. "You're a free man." But Jeremiah also felt a vague dissatisfaction. He'd always meant to say something to the counselor about calling him Jerry.

As soon as he was finished with the counselor, he'd started looking for a woman. They'd covered women in the little sessions. The counselor would lean across the desk, a twinkle in his eye, a nudge in the elbow, saying, "It's the women, isn't it, Jerry? They're something, huh? Missed them? Dreams? Fantasies?" He'd acted like they were two men on a bus, watching the legs get on and off. "You still a virgin, Jerry?" Now they'd descended from the bus, into the locker room, where boys teased one another about their experience.

After a brief courtship Jeremiah and Betty had been married by a justice of the peace. Betty wasn't Catholic, and Jeremiah hadn't wanted to insist that she go through the conversion process. The people at the office gave them a shower with lots of Tupperware and Corningware and a set of stainless-steel silverware. They were set up. Betty had everything a person could need for a house, since she'd been waiting for years to get married, so it didn't matter that Jeremiah's household was so meager. He'd never gotten the hang of domesticity like some of the other priests from the old days. He'd always been an office person. So he was happy to get someone like Betty, who knew how things should run and look in their house.

They could afford a house, in fact, because Betty had saved for the past ten years for her wedding, and when it turned out to be just the two of them and Floyd as a witness, they'd taken her sizable savings account and put it as a down payment on a place of their own. Jeremiah liked to think that Betty came equipped, like a backpacker ready to survive in the wilderness. Towels appeared in the bathroom, soap in the soap dishes, sheets on the bed, even a hanging plant here and there—all assurances that Jeremiah had been right in his choice of a plain woman. And at night he climbed aboard and performed the acts he'd seen and read about and heard discussed.

Now, five years later, Betty was leaving him notes taped to the television screen and disappearing. As Jeremiah settled into his comfortable easy chair for the evening's television with a sandwich and beer assembled on the little table next to him, he began to think that maybe all the trouble had started when the old black-and-white cabinet had replaced the color television Floyd had finally recaptured. It was as if an irritant, nettles, had been introduced onto the skin of their relationship. Things that hadn't bothered Betty before seemed to pop up like itchy places she scratched and dug at. Jeremiah ate his sandwich slowly, chewing carefully to the rhythm of the music overlaid on the screen in front of him.

Day Two

Jeremiah woke up at six o'clock in the morning to the sound of the doorbell. But when he went to the front door, an easy few steps from the chair he'd slept in all night in front of the television, no one was there. That made sense. After all, it was only six, according to the glue-on digital clock Betty had fastened to the control side of the television. Jeremiah looked at the screen for a few sleepy moments before he realized that the gray white haze was not going to resolve itself into a scene. The station was off the air. He reached over and snapped it off, but he continued to stand in front of it, his eyes caught by the growing pile of yellow lined papers with Betty's familiar bad typing.

Then he realized that the reason he was still in the living room with the television on at six in the morning was that Betty hadn't come home that night. At least, he assumed she hadn't. He moved slowly toward the bedroom, not sure he wanted to certify that fact. Sure enough, the bed, perfectly made every day by Betty, was untouched. No Betty. Jeremiah debated for a moment whether he should take off his clothes and try to get some real sleep before work or just go ahead and get ready a bit early.

He didn't want Betty to find him sleeping when she got home. He wasn't sure why. In fact, as he soaped himself with Betty's special cinnamon soap, no matter that he felt like a breakfast item on the menu, he decided that he didn't know how he was supposed to feel about this. He tried to imagine how someone on television would feel. He knew that he might be angry with Betty for staying out all night and, for all he knew, carrying on with someone else: another man. But he might also be worried, call hospitals, police, friends.

As he rubbed his stomach and groin area with the soap, he felt a roughness on the soap's surface, ridges that hadn't previously been there. Stepping out of the stream of water and blinking several times to clear his eyes, he examined the soap carefully. A crude heart had been carved into the tan surface. The sides around it had been dug away so the heart stood out in the middle. The jagged edges left by the knife made it seem that the heart had sprouted hair or was about to come apart. Betty.

He looked around for another bar of soap but couldn't see any. He hated to use this one again for some reason. Superstition. On educational television, they talked a lot about subjects like that, how it seemed that people were controlled by superstition and fear more than anything else. Jeremiah picked up the soap, feeling the ridge of heart in his palm, and finished the soaping of his legs and feet, working the suds in between each toe.

Fixing his own breakfast wasn't a big deal, Jeremiah thought, as he ate. Usually Betty had everything ready to go by the time he was out of the shower and dressed, but since he was up early, he had time to do it all himself. The only problem had been finding the pigeon in the freezer. He'd forgotten about that: a month ago Betty found it dead on the sidewalk and brought it home. At least, that's what she told him. She carefully sealed it in a Ziploc plastic bag and placed it in the freezer. When he opened the door to get the can of orange juice, the pigeon glowed a soft violet light at him. He almost picked it up before he remembered that it was the pigeon. Later, while he ate, he realized he'd never asked her why it was in the freezer. He knew Betty must have a good answer, like a contestant on a game show, and since she always did things for a good reason, he almost never asked her why about anything.

Work was the same as always, except for lunch. He'd forgotten that Betty always made bag lunches for them. So at eleven-thirty he opened the drawer where he kept the bag and for a moment was confused when it was empty. He looked up and around to ask Betty about it and then realized that she wasn't around and he'd forgotten about it himself. Luckily he had enough money to take himself down to the lunch counter on the main floor of the building. He'd forgotten how good their soup was and fully enjoyed the experience.

Once in the middle of the afternoon his concentration on his typing was broken by a small commotion to the left of him, a scurry of voices and figures. One person looked familiar. He decided later it must have been Betty. He'd spent so much time with her that now when he tried to call up her face, he had difficulty. Plain, yes, but how? He'd grown used to seeing her in pieces, he decided. That was the problem. And now he couldn't put her together. It was like watching the old black-and-white at home: gradually channels pitched and rolled like small boats on a rough sea, stopping for periods of time just out of square, legs or heads cut off, people and scenes elongated or flattened. Some channels wouldn't come in at all. Though he could hear the dialogue perfectly, the picture was a jumble of lines. Now he was down to just one channel that worked all of the time.

The women in the typing pool had gone back to talking about him as if he weren't there, he noticed, now that Betty wasn't around to protect him. All afternoon he caught snatches of conversation like an outfielder but never hurled them back. Apparently everyone knew something he didn't know about Betty, and the fact that he didn't or couldn't or hadn't was a sign of something else. As it was, he typed more and more slowly as the afternoon wore on, in his efforts to make sense out of things.

When the supervisor came by at four-fifteen to check the work, she just shook her head at the tiny output in his basket, gave him a sharp look, and passed on to the next desk. Ordinarily Jeremiah would have felt a twinge of shame over such a performance, but today he felt somehow justified and would have said so had anyone bothered to ask him. But no one did. When he realized that that wasn't unusual, that almost no one spoke to him but always spoke to Betty, he felt another twinge. This time he couldn't readily name it. So at the end of the day as he put on his coat with the rest of the workers, he tried to nod and speak to a couple of other people whose desks were next to his. They just looked at him, like startled birds, and walked off toward the elevator.

In the parking lot he waited for Betty to drive the car around and pick him up as always, then realized he would have to take the bus home because he had taken it to work that morning. Betty had the car, wherever she was.

The bus was actually more pleasant than he remembered from the pre-Betty days, when he hadn't had a car. The priests leaving the order could put in for such a nicety if they had had a parish or had been good fund-raisers in some capacity, but since Jeremiah had only been a clerk-typist, he'd known better than to even ask. Still, as he rode along, the voice of Father Denton, who'd trained him in, kept coming back. "That's the trouble with women," he said, as the bus crossed Fifth and made the loop through the downtown stops. "They thrive on confusion, complication. They *love* trouble!"

Jeremiah had always nodded agreement whenever the old priest had started in on one of his diatribes against some group or another. He tried to humor him. After all, he didn't want to end up on the Iron Range in northern Minnesota. The old man had that kind of power, for some reason. Everyone in the Twin Cities diocese was conscious of his power. Father Denton could send a man anywhere he chose after seminary, and oftentimes even later. One word from the old man and you'd be sent packing. "We'll send this one off to Fargo. Let the cold and dust settle him down. He'll come back with the starch taken out." He'd wink and nod as he signed the paper with a sweep of his hand. Jeremiah knew about these shifts because he had remained to become the old man's clerk after finishing his seminary courses. Although he'd thought a bit about parish work, he'd never really pursued it. Besides, the old man had plucked him out before he even had a chance. Jeremiah had felt relieved that the decision was out of his hands. Following dutifully the path set by his mentor, he had put his fingers on the IBM Selectric and never strayed.

Now, in this current problem with Betty, though, Jeremiah worried that maybe the old man had been right. He tried to take his mind off Denton's voice and tried to remember a conversation, any conversation he'd ever had with Betty—something to lock in her voice. But he couldn't. He couldn't recall a single one, just a blur of single words and phrases. Maybe the old man should have sent him to International Falls or Hibbing when he'd wanted to leave—anything rather than nod and smile and sign the paper with a sweep of the hand. As the bus toiled out of downtown toward the neat houses and lawns of the suburbs, Jeremiah realized that that had always bothered him. Father Denton had never tried to talk him out of leaving, had never done the fatherly thing—putting his arm around his shoulders, seating him on the leather sofa in his office, and counseling him about the meaning of their life, their commitment. Jeremiah had felt disappointed about missing that moment and worried that maybe the old man had been trying to tell him that he should leave, that he wasn't cut out for their life. "How would you ever know for sure?" he wanted to ask the old priest, but he could already see the shake of the head and the smile.

As the bus rounded Lyly Park, Jeremiah realized that in fact he'd been hurt because Father Denton had not fought for him to stay. He had assigned him to the world without a struggle, sending him out and away as if he were some kind of Judas, rather than the man who'd been faithful in his service for ten years. When the time had come, Jeremiah wasn't even worth fighting for. For a moment he tried to convince himself that he was mistaken, that the old priest was senile, that he was incompetent—that's why he had let Jeremiah go. But as the bus slowed to Jeremiah's stop at the corner of Pierce and Ashland, he had to admit that Father Denton must have known exactly what he was doing. It was the same smile and sweep of the hand over the paper that Jeremiah had watched all those years, sending men out to meet their doom.

On the front steps of the house Jeremiah found a four-pack of toilet paper, the extra soft, two-ply kind they advertised on television, that he particularly liked. Just inside the front door, toppled over like a pyramid display in the grocery store, oranges were scattered through the entryway, a few still rolling down the hallway to the kitchen.

"Betty?" he called. "Betty? Betty, are you here?" As he listened, he thought he heard the hushed sigh of the back door pulled into place. Then silence. He stood for a moment, confused, then walked quickly, almost on tiptoe, to the kitchen. There in the middle of the floor lay a split bag of groceries, leaking a carton of eggs, an overturned quart of milk, and Wheaties, the breakfast of champions.

That night Jeremiah watched television again, struggling to bring in more than the single channel, until he fell asleep and again woke up at dawn, to the mysterious dong of the bell. This time he didn't bother to answer the door but went immediately to the bathroom to shower with the bar of soap whose etched heart seemed to dig cruelly into his skin. "Betty, oh, Betty," he sighed.

Day Three

After clicking the black-and-white on, waiting for the creamy pool of light to spread, Jeremiah noticed that the notes on top of the television were gone. Moreover, there had been no note taped to the screen for two days

now. Then he turned to the good channel, to a wrestling program, and settled into his chair, a beer and
sandwich on the table next to him. When he'd come
home that evening after another strange day at work—
with little glimpses of Betty popping up along the frin-
ges of his vision, the women around him talking more
and more openly, their words like penknives they
would gladly attack him with—he'd found cookies,
chocolate-chip, fresh-baked, on aluminum foil cooling
on the kitchen counter. Later he'd have some, after he
gave the beer a chance to work and his stomach time to
calm from the tension that had been building in him
since morning.

On the bus, when Father Denton's voice had made its appearance again, he'd had to fight to keep from yelling out at
that old betrayer, that old breaker of men's spirits. All those
years of listening to that crap for nothing. Betty. If only he
could tune in her voice instead. He'd have to find her, bring
her back, talk to her, he decided.

The problem was, though, that the minute he hit the front
steps of the house the impulse was sucked out of him. By the
time his hand was on the knob, turning it, he felt the draw of
the living room, the hush and promise of the easy chair, and
the peace of the television. It was all he could do to keep from
stumbling over the letters and circulars that had spilled
through the mail slot onto the floor of the entryway.

He didn't hear the back door this time or feel Betty's
presence in the house. There was nothing except the bare
ticking of furniture and appliances. Stepping over the pile of
mail, Jeremiah had gone to the bedroom to change clothes.
The bed was still made, as it had been three days ago when
all this started. But in the middle of the bed lay a small brown
object. Picking it up and turning it over a few times, Jeremiah
finally recognized it: the rubber heel from a shoe, worn off at
one edge from sloppy walking. Turning it over again, he

noticed the symmetry of the nail holes punched at neat intervals and the faint outline of printed letters, RIS, but nothing else. He remembered how when he was a boy, the shoes with rubber heels had been embossed with a cat showing a paw, and when his shoes were new or resoled, he could go stamping through mud or water and leave a neat imprint on the sidewalk or mark his mother's floor. He shook his head and put the fragment of heel back on the middle of the bed. Now wasn't the time to disturb anything.

The wrestling match between Ezra the Weasel and Bobby the Ladder was moving slowly, resembling a clumsy vaudeville routine in slow motion. The Weasel crouched down and scurried out under the ropes every time the Ladder got near enough to use force. The cameraman was also getting restless, and, amid the boos and bored hoots he began to pan the faces of the audience.

Then a face like Betty's filled the screen of the television, causing Jeremiah to leap up out of his chair as if he were being called to attention. She was looking at the wrestlers, and the camera held on her. She seemed to be saying something, but the sound wasn't coming through. Then she was gone, and the screen was flashing with other faces yelling and shaking fists in the air at the antics of the Weasel and the Ladder.

Jeremiah stood for a minute more, then returned to his chair, sitting tensely on the edge in case the face should appear again.

When the wrestling was over, Jeremiah leaned back exhausted. He had not seen Betty again. Although he'd thought he might have spotted her once in about the seventh row, he really couldn't be certain. At the break between programs he went to the kitchen and grabbed a handful of cookies and another beer from the fridge, remembering that he'd forgotten to buy beer, so Betty must have. This time he caught sight of what he must have missed the first time he opened the door: the pigeon had been moved from the freezer to the lower part of the refrigerator. She must be defrosting it, he thought, and he closed the door on the violet breast winking satin light out at him.

Private Lives

IT WAS ONLY a matter of time. At least that's what Albert told Frederick. It was okay for Albert to hire the boys and insist that they dress in their cotton, church-blue pants and long-sleeved white shirts. White set off the innocent glow of their faces and the small dirty moons of nails on their delicate twelve-year-old hands. That was okay. Teach them to move softly between the chairs and tables, to inquire discreetly over the customer's left shoulder for coffee, tea, water.

Albert liked to watch them hesitate, straining with the plastic pitcher he insisted they keep filled to the brim with almost cool tap water. Handling it as if it were heirloom crystal, they paused, sliding the left hand under the bottom as if it were a small animal slipping from their grasp, then remembering his instructions, withdrawing and placing the hand behind the back again. Then they would right themselves, and straining to lift and angle the pitcher exactly, they would pour the water expertly into the glass.

Albert liked to watch the down at the back of their necks prickle with the strain and the small unlined faces wrinkle like a bedsheet suddenly grabbed in a fist and then let go again. There was nothing like that. When he looked at his own face in the mirror, he knew what was wrong with it.

When he pulled at the skin pooling under his eyes, it took too long to return and sometimes stood up like an ocean wave until he patted it back in place.

"There's nothing you can do about it now," Albert told Frederick later as they lay in bed, stiff and familiar as man and wife after years of struggle. They had not caved in to the desire to sleep separately but had bought a huge, king-size bed instead. Now each lay marooned on his side, avoiding the imaginary line that bisected their nights, like the sword of Damocles, Albert thought. Frederick worried that somehow the box springs, which were two separate twin beds, would part like the *Titanic* one night and strand them permanently or toss them into the smothering ocean of covers on the floor. When Frederick told him about it, Albert tapped the ashes off his cigarette, put his book down with a sigh, and stood up on the bed.

"What're you doing?" Frederick demanded, as he pulled away from the chasm that at any moment could erupt in the middle. But Albert just marched around, sending Frederick out of bed in a scramble that pulled most of the covers off with him. "Watch what you're doing there."

Albert grinned meanly and bounced his six-foot-one height close to the ceiling.

"Hey," Frederick cried out. "Stop it! Do you want to go through the floor or something?" He tried to pull around him some of the blankets they had piled on for the bitter January cold of Minnesota, but Albert's antics had left them on the far corner. Albert's face was turning red in the effort of his gymnastics, and Frederick knew he'd better do something before he hurt himself. Really, he had almost no sense at all.

"All right, you made your point." Frederick made himself smile and grabbed at Albert's legs.

When they'd met in Chicago so many years ago, Frederick couldn't get enough of those beautiful long legs. He made Albert take off everything but his boxers in the apartment and strut around, even though the windows were open and his neighbors across the courtyard were peering around the corners of their curtains at the "two fags" across the way. Frederick smarted under their disapproval and held on tightly to Albert despite the early troubles.

It was like "Jack and the Beanstalk" in the late afternoon when Albert would come back to clean up and rest before the evening rush at the hotel. Frederick felt like Jack wanting to and then doing it – climbing those legs like a stairway to the sky. Then Albert's beautiful white length would be stretched across the double bed that seemed too big to them. They could hardly get close enough, as Frederick ran his tongue up and around the calves, licking the salty smooth down and the milky skin his Czech parents had given Albert. "Why don't you ever tan?" Frederick asked him once, but Albert looked at him as if he was crazy. Later Frederick would come to realize that in the Old World a man with a tan worked outside, was a peasant, and that Albert's family had always struggled to keep their boys inside, in trades, away from peasant life. Twenty years later, when Albert discovered he was going to get old, he spent months in a tanning parlor, basting and turning like a Thanksgiving turkey, but he got old anyway. That's when he started dating.

"What do you mean, you're going out?" Frederick demanded.

"There's this boy who works for me – well, for the hotel. A busboy." Albert buttered his English muffin carefully, trimming the sides with the knife as if he were decorating one of his petits fours.

"A boy? A busboy?"

When Albert nodded and took his first bite, tentatively, the way he tasted all food, checking for flavor and texture the way he tasted all food, checking for flavor and texture even of the items he wasn't involved in preparing, Frederick slammed his fork down on the white Formica in the breakfast nook.

"Now, Frederick, blood pressure, right?" Albert reminded him and took a larger second bite of the muffin. It was perfect. Just the way the busboy was. Puerto Rican, tan, muscular. He noticed the way Frederick, older by three years, was beginning to lose muscle tone, or maybe his skin was getting gray with his hair. Something. Frederick was trying to stare down Albert's inspecting gaze. Pushed back against the wood of the booth, he looked as if he might hurt himself, bruise something, if he didn't relax.

How can you? Just tell me that we've . . . well, we've . . . What about last night? This morning in the shower? 'I love you forever?' What does that mean?"

Albert put down the muffin and took a sip of Frederick's coffee, made the way Albert had taught him. In fact, Albert had taught him everything about cooking, and more, a lot more. He put that knowledge in his eyes and stared hard at Frederick. "It means I have a date. I'm going out tonight after work. The kid gets off at eleven. We're just going for a couple of drinks. He's been trying to come out for a month now. I just want to talk to him. Guys at work give him the cold shoulder or a load of shit. They don't trust him. He's a good kid, though. Really. Takes care of his mother and sister. Puerto Ricans have strong family ties, like the Ukrainians do." He added the last part for Frederick, who couldn't stand being hugged by the fat Ukrainian aunts smelling of sweat and yeast from their hours of baking in the kitchen, with their hair a flat helmet from the scarves they wore. The women in Frederick's family were beautiful, educated. They never touched you with more than a fingertip, and they kissed the air on either side of your face whenever they met you.

The business of their families was always a problem, well, after the first few months, when they were so dizzy in love they barely had time to work and sleep. Each day a new surprise. Special dishes Albert would prepare at the Drake Hotel's expense and bring home at one in the morning for their feasts. The tiny gifts Frederick would buy to quietly please Albert, who neither shopped nor could afford to shop on his beginning salary as under-under-under chef. Long hours and short pay—but none of that mattered. They would barely have time to eat the glorious dishes—slices of beef Wellington, little pastry birds stuffed with crab—before they would be in the bedroom, then later on the sofa in the living room, on the rug in front of the fireplace, and later on the kitchen table, on the floor of the bathroom, sick with desire, sick with love. Although they ate wonderfully, they lost weight with love—the shudder of a hand sliding up an arm, the careful strokes sponging the kitchen smells from Albert's limbs, the slow massage of the shampoo, Albert leaning tiredly and happily back into the bowl of Frederick's arms as they waited out the night in the soothing water of the huge tub.

Now he has a date, Frederick thought. Now. The wink of the ruby ring he'd given Albert seemed like a lewd gesture after all those years. Now?

When the first tears appeared, Frederick fought them. He wasn't going to give in to Albert this time. He was going to fight him as though the playground bully was sitting on his chest yelling, "Give, give."

Then he felt tired suddenly, the way he always felt with the bully. He'd finally say uncle, aunt, whatever they wanted, and feel the sudden relief of their weight lifted from his chest. Looking toward home, he'd pick up his things, clutch them tightly to cover the hole in his chest, and trudge across the playground to the corner exit space torn in the fence. By the time he reached home, he'd be too exhausted to do anything but go quietly to his room and collapse on the bed.

Though he'd just gotten up and showered on the morning Albert made his announcement and though he had a class to teach at the university, Frederick knew he'd have to go back to bed. He couldn't even think.

"God, I knew you'd do this." Albert banged his mug on the table.

"I can't . . ." Frederick found he couldn't talk. His feelings landed in his throat like a fist. He got up carefully, in slow motion like the old people in his family, put the napkin carefully by the plate with the *D* for the Drake Hotel in a scrolled silver monogram at the edge. Albert had insisted that they use the plates and silverware he took from the job. It became a curiosity among their friends, who knew that by now the couple could afford better.

"He's over eighteen, Frederick. He's not jailbait." Albert rose and threw his napkin across the table at the space Frederick had just vacated. "I'm probably not going to do anything, anyway. Really." He followed Frederick out of the kitchen and down the hallway to their bedroom. "I just need a couple of drinks to unwind after cooking. You know how it is."

Frederick stopped and turned. "Of course." And they both saw those long-ago nights when Albert would come rushing home to Frederick's champagne and nakedness.

Frederick could feel the weight of exhaustion settle over him like a collapsing tent. He wasn't a good camper. "Have to call school, can't go." He could feel his language, his sentences slipping away from him as he reached for the phone.

By the time he got the history-department secretary, he sounded as sick as he claimed he was. "Hope you feel better soon," she was saying as he hung up the receiver. Albert knelt down at the foot of the bed and slid off Frederick's loafers and socks. He worked gently and efficiently, undressing Frederick as if he were a tired child carried in from the car after a big day.

As Frederick drifted off that morning, to blanket-warm brown sleep and safety, Albert kissed him on the top of his head and whispered, "I'm sorry." Sometime in his sleep Frederick heard a door slam, and then it was dark and he was awake. Nine o'clock. Albert was at the hotel. Or Frederick supposed he was. As head chef, he had to be. There with another man.

Frederick felt as if he'd slept himself out of time. Now he couldn't go back to the morning. He couldn't explain or ask questions. Albert had launched himself to another planet, and Frederick could only stand and watch mutely when Albert didn't come home that night, when he didn't come home for several nights in a row. Frederick felt like an astronomer scanning deep space for something unknown, something unnamed he knew he'd recognize.

Then there were periods of relative calm, and Albert and Frederick slipped back into their old patterns as if nothing had changed. But when Frederick held Albert's cock in his hand, it felt foreign now, not an instrument of love, just an instrument, a specialty tool on the operating table, sterilized, used by others. It had entered other mouths, other . . . It took all of Frederick's concentration not to imagine what Albert did out there at night. It took all of the discipline that had driven him through graduate school, through the books and articles he had to publish to survive at the University of Chicago, through his stint as chairman of the department when it was filled with eccentrics who warred like tribes over food in a drought.

When he kissed Albert, his tongue tracing the polish of each tooth, he sometimes felt like a Marine recruit, given a job to do that was totally without meaning, fruitless, like digging a hole just to fill it up again. He found other tastes in that mouth, or he imagined he did. Where had they come from?

New toothpaste? What he drank or ate in love late at night?

There had been little acts of retaliation: the amnesia that took over when he made coffee for Albert and the refusal to make the pilgrimage home for holidays to St. Paul and to rest uneasily in the dark overstuffed comfort of the living room sofa while Albert slept upstairs in his boyhood bed in the room saved for him from high school, full of the trophies electroplated with gold finish for every kind of sport.

Albert called him at Christmas. "They miss you," he breathed into the distance, while Frederick blinked the lights of Chicago's celebration into single huge bulbs of red and green tears. "They keep asking why you didn't come."

"What did you tell them?"

"I don't know. I made something up."

"What about the truth? You know—you're fucking around."

Albert sighed, as good a sigh as Frederick might have given. "Don't start now. Please?"

For once Albert sounded as though he meant it, so Frederick nodded at the wind-blown lights in the street below, then said, "Okay. Merry Christmas." What followed sounded like an explosion of laughter, until Frederick realized it was sobbing, sobbing loud enough to wake the parents and aunts.

"Shhh, hush, Albert. God, be quiet, hon. They'll hear you. Albert? Albert?" Suddenly none of the past months mattered, nor the year before. Frederick only wanted to be there, to hold his lover, to kiss the teared eyes before he had a chance to change again.

"I'm so, so, so sorrry . . . sorry. God, I can't believe . . . God, Freddy, please don't—"

"No, no, it's okay. I'm not going to leave. Really, hang on, Ally. Please, don't cry so loudly. They'll hear you and come down." Frederick was fighting the weight of tiredness himself, but he figured he had to pay attention.

"No, you have to forgive me. I fucked us up, and I do love you. None of the others count. How could they? I don't know what's the matter. I just get crazy and have to have it. I can't stop myself now. I try, I try, and then something happens, and I . . . God, I'm sorry, Freddy. I don't see how you can stand me."

Frederick would always remember the three-hour session of self-loathing and apology. It saved them in one way. Later, while Albert was in therapy but still having affairs, Frederick would use that moment to keep himself from packing the suitcases he had gathered from the closets around their apartment. Actually, he was so stubborn that he wasn't going to leave. He was going to make Albert leave. But then he knew that that wouldn't, couldn't happen. Albert could never live alone. He'd always need someone to be there when he got home. That thought once made Frederick so angry that he went to the kitchen and smashed all the Drake Hotel plates, cups, saucers, and bowls. As if that wasn't enough, he got out a chisel and started gouging out the script *D* engraved in the handles of the silverware. While he worked, he played Frank Sinatra records real loud. "Did it my way," he sang along as he tried to avoid the sharp edge of the chisel with his fingers.

When Albert came home the next morning to find Frederick slumped over asleep at the breakfast nook, in a sea of smashed dishes and with the silver curls of metal scattered about him like rain, he realized something had to give. So Albert packed himself and was gone before Frederick woke up and found his note and saw that the toothpaste was missing from the medicine cabinet.

"Jesus Christ," he swore as he mixed the baking soda and salt in the plastic mug he found in the corner of the top cabinet. "Now what? I've got this meeting with the provost, no goddamn toothpaste, and my hands look like I've been doing heavy leather all night."

A month later Albert started dropping by at breakfast. Usually he didn't even appear to have stayed up all night. Frederick didn't put himself out, just gestured toward the coffeepot and smiled when Albert discovered how Frederick liked his coffee now.

There were no more tears, just the hidden misty eyes a few months later as they said goodbye to Chicago and the Drake and their apartment. Both men were silent as they drove their new car north to Wisconsin and into Minnesota.

Putting the bed back together was the kind of domestic ritual that usually annoyed Albert. He refused to change sheets weekly, sometimes even monthly, so Frederick had to struggle with it alone most of the time. In fact, only a real tantrum convinced Albert of the need for the Sears washer and dryer Frederick bought and had delivered. Jesus, what will the Sears guys think? Frederick wondered when Albert ran out in his socks to the wet street, waving his arms and hollering, "Stop, stop it's not ours! Stop!"

"Of course it is," Frederick told him. "Stop being an ass. I ordered them. Cheap, Sears, see? We need to do the laundry, for Christ's sake." The two delivery men stood in the back of the truck, hands on their hips, snickering at the two nannies in their soaked socks, now glued with fallen leaves.

When Albert noticed the two guys laughing, he wanted a fight, but he shrugged and turned away. It was his old family neighborhood in St. Paul. He couldn't shame them here. "I just thought you could walk across the street to the laundromat. For God's sake, it's just across the street." Then he clumped back into the building and up the stairs, leaving a trail of sticky orange leaves from the maples the city had planted out front when the elms had started dying ten years before. Frederick remembered the worn black linoleum of each step marked by an orange blob.

As they tucked in the blankets now, each man at a corner of the king-size mattress, Albert stopped and rubbed the small of his back. A spasm of pain crossed his face.

"I knew it," Frederick said.

"Oh, be quiet. You always say that. 'I knew it.'" Albert bent slowly back, then rotated clockwise from his hips to loosen the muscles that were grabbing. "What haven't you known? You're such a predictor, aren't you. Such a know-it-all." Though it sounded mean, Albert grinned and smacked his lips into a kiss that might even have been a come-on.

Frederick smiled and wondered if Albert wanted to snuggle a bit. Lately they'd lain in bed like Albert's two ancient aunts, side by side, framed by pillows and covers, looking out with the expression of two survivors in a rowboat at sea, expecting the worst. "I guess there's some things I wasn't too good at," Frederick said.

Albert gave the top down comforter a hard jerk, pulling it momentarily from Frederick's grip. "Hey."

"Sorry." Albert stopped and watched Frederick resettle the pale blue comforter back squarely on the bed. He hated that damn thing, thought it unnecessary, like the washer and dryer. But Frederick had to have a lot of covers. He'd live there with Albert but only on certain conditions: they had to keep warm, and they had to get to know some other couples — no more single men who kept Frederick bird-nervous through dinner. Albert laughed to himself. Maybe he should have listened to Frederick sooner.

Positioned back in bed, Albert picked up his book, then set it down again. "Are you hungry?"

"Well, maybe just a bite of something. What's in there?" Frederick always left the food business to Albert, and he never complained at the extravagance he noticed in the kitchens, either their small one or the restaurant-size one on the main floor below, where Albert ran his Continental-style café.

Albert smiled and put the book back on the antique sewing table that served as a nightstand beside the bed. Then impulsively he leaned over and kissed Frederick's surprised lips softly, not exactly with passion but much more tenderly than their usual peck hello and goodbye. "Be back in a minute."

Frederick leaned back, watching Albert climb carefully out of bed, straighten stiffly, and walk with a slight limp out of the room. Albert's years of cooking long hours at the Drake had damaged the disks in his back. Frederick glanced down at the book he had been about to open. Those damn French. Just when he'd thought there weren't that many surprises left in his field, the French set off this time bomb. Now they'd have to figure things out all over again. His department at the college wanted to ignore the French. "Just forget it," they advised him. "Who gives a shit. No one ever takes the French seriously, anyway, a bunch of drunks."

Frederick hadn't even considered their comments. He'd come from the University of Chicago, where a scholar didn't ignore breakthrough work, whether by the French or not. For a few years he'd felt, in fact, that something was happening. Phillipe Aries was not a fly-by-night, although it irritated him that Aries got big play in the bookstores. Frederick's books sat in libraries and on his own shelves, unnoticed after the initial response from the scholarly community. Now he was just a footnote in graduate-student papers.

The French based their work on ordinary people, not on highly visible events and powerful figures. Frederick could see the merit. He was picking up a lot reading *The History of Private Lives, Volume I: Roman to Byzantine*. These guys had really done their homework, and they wrote in a conversational style, and he couldn't begin to write that way.

What was keeping Albert? He must have decided to whip up something special. Frederick hoped he hadn't gone downstairs and started mucking around in the restaurant, because he'd be up all night rearranging the menu again, adding and deleting items he'd be testing on the big stoves and ovens. When he cooked, Albert became as absorbed as an artist or a scholar. The only difference was that he usually needed an assistant. Maybe he was more like a chemist, like that guy from 3M they'd met a few weeks ago. The problem was that Frederick couldn't stand to help him, and the helpers Albert hired never lasted very long. Trained by his twenty-five years in hotel kitchens, Albert was demanding, autocratic, bad-tempered. There was no other way to say it: he was Rudolph Hess in the kitchen. To work with him was excruciating. You never made the right move. You always got berated for the slightest mistake, and the whole thing usually escalated until the assistant left.

They'd had to close the restaurant early some nights because Albert had driven off the help. Some days they couldn't open until Frederick phoned from his office and negotiated with the help, while Albert sulked in the corner under the plastic grapes and vinery his mother and aunts kept trailing in from their days of shopping discount stores and closeouts.

Frederick couldn't imagine how the customers stood it, either. Albert insulted them, kept them waiting to be seated even when the restaurant was empty, and warned them that it would be hours before the food would appear. Some people were frightened off, but those who had been there before just smiled, nodded, and sat down, knowing that the food would appear, heaped generously on the Drake Hotel plates and tasting wonderful. Although he claimed to serve Continental cuisine, it was always the hearty Czech, German, and Polish dishes of his family's tradition that Albert prepared for the specials.

Albert was kind only to the old men of the neighborhood. They were mostly widowers, although some were bachelors who had spent their lives with their families and eventually lived alone in the little frame workers' houses that lined the streets fanning out from the brewery, whose huge smoke-stack and neon sign glowed over the lives on the river flats like a benediction. Most of the immigrants had given their lives to the long lines of bottles rolling train-smooth to ma-chines that cleaned and filled and capped and loaded them into cases. Now the men walked slowly with bent backs and hearts of retirement. Or they visited one another at their porches or garages all summer day. The women walked about the neighborhood in their housedresses, thick-heeled shoes and babushkas and gathered under the awnings of the restaurant on the first floor of the three-story brick building, which housed Frederick and Albert on the second floor and the Ukrainian Hall on the third floor.

When the mornings were mild and pleasant, Frederick slept in and dreamed, through their murmurings, of spend-ing childhood vacations in the country, where the constant hum of insects, the call of birds, and the swish of trees had made him sleepy all the time. He'd felt his heart slow and pump with satisfaction then.

Sometimes Frederick wondered what the neighborhood thought of them, living together at their age, men in their late fifties without women. But there was the tradition of bach-elors. Albert's kindness to these men seemed to testify to an instinct of upbringing more than anything else. Each man had his particular table and timing. They never had to wait to be seated or to receive food. Often they never even had to order. Albert locked them into the grid of a memory that had kept the massive kitchens of the Drake running smoothly through thousands of recipes and eccentric demands. Tak-ing care of a few old men in worn brown and olive clothes was simple. Other customers waited while Albert poured second and third cups of strong coffee, brought their familiar plates of food, and added a free cookie or cake. Albert never flirted with these men. He was a man among men, his voice deep and regular, his gestures economical.

With others it was different. Frederick had to watch himself when he was down there, because seeing Albert's fingers brush the shoulder of another man or cock his head and say something caustic, full of double entendres as thick as the raisins in his rice pudding, made Frederick crazy. He wanted to hit him, throw the dishes on the floor again. It wouldn't do any good with the silverware. Albert had decided that it was a fine idea to gouge the *D* out. Frederick had spent nightmare hours after that, cutting his fingers as he chipped silver tears out of the handles of everything Albert brought home. After twenty-five years they could stock a restaurant.

Thank God, at least that part was over. Frederick put the book on the floor beside him and scooted down in the covers, pulling them up to his chin. His foot touched the side of the bed, and he decided to move over, spread out, luxuriate as long as Albert was gone for a few moments. From the middle he could spread-eagle, and even though he was on the fault line of the twin boxes below, he felt light and safe there.

When the thought of the French came back, he shrugged. So what. There was always going to be something new. That's what attracted him to history to begin with, right? Old and new. His work in the classics was pure pleasure because of that paradox. Maybe the French had an angle he could use. A full professor, turning sixty next summer, he knew his colleagues were waiting for him to hit retirement and leave. But he had some news for them: Not at sixty-five, which they figured he could afford. Not at seventy, which up until last year had been mandatory. And if he worked the French angle somehow, not until he dropped dead in the classroom, a piece of chalk in one hand, the slide-projector remote in the other. By God, he'd outlive and outteach all of them. He just needed to get going on this French thing.

Frederick was dozing off when the clank of dishes announced Albert's arrival back from the kitchen. "Still hungry?" Albert smiled and stood beside the bed, his arms full of things: a huge tray he must have gone downstairs to get, five covered plates, wineglasses, a loaf of French bread teetering across the top, a sherbet glass of chocolate mousse, another of something pink that wobbled, and a bottle of wine under each arm, champagne and French red. "Don't just stand there," Albert said, and Frederick crawled out of the covers to help him.

Later, with the remnants of the food and dishes spread around them, Albert reached down to the bottle of champagne chilling beside the bed on the floor. He slid the wine smoothly into the crystal champagne flutes Frederick had bought because he'd wanted one thing that hadn't been used by a thousand lips before his. Handing a glass to Frederick, Albert sat a bit straighter, cleared his throat, and said, "It hasn't been that bad, has it? I mean, regardless of what is going to . . . well, you know, I've always loved just you, Freddy." Frederick smiled, and they nudged their glasses and drank.

Later still, after their lovemaking, which took a long time because it had been such a long time, the shower had felt good. Rubbing their tired muscles for each other, ignoring the bellies and buttocks that sagged now and the way the skin behind their ears had gotten old while they weren't looking, they had felt something different come over them.

"Maybe I shouldn't hire another kid," Albert said softly into the darkness of their room, lit now only by the slice of moon that hung outside their windows like a rind in a glass of night sky. He sighed and rolled closer to Frederick. "Nothing's safe anymore, I mean. What if — "

"Don't worry so much," Frederick said, stretching his legs wide again, then rubbing his toes up the length of Albert's long calf.

"Don't." Albert shifted irritably. "No, this way. Roll over. Yeah, like that. Let me hug you, yeah, there." And Albert pulled Frederick's smaller, rounder body into the lean cup of his own. "Anyway, I'm not just worrying." Albert wrapped his arms more tightly around Frederick's body and grabbed his own wrists in front, as if he were going to perform a rescue in deep water. "Face it, our friends, people we used to know in Chicago, are dying, Freddy." Albert felt Frederick's body stiffen, and he held on even harder.

"No." Frederick groaned and pushed against the embrace of Albert's arms and the grip of Albert's leg thrown over him.

"Yes," Albert whispered, as he kissed the gray hair of Frederick's head softly. "Yes." He kissed the curious loose skin at the jaw line and rested his mouth where the pulse pushed lightly against the rough hide of Frederick's throat.

The Only Thing Different

EVERY TIME his voice tumbles down the hall and around the corner into the bathroom at her, she takes another swipe. The hair sprinkles the sink like pine needles, curved slivers of heart.

When the sink is filled with red brown, she gathers up the hair and puts handfuls of it in the blue plastic wastebasket. "You just don't realize that you're being selfish. That's the problem." He calls from the bedroom, where he is getting ready.

Selfish? she thinks, as she pulls out a curly lock and straightens it between her fingers. Stand up and be counted. The scissors cut deeply, and her hair remains stiff with its top lopped off and falling silently in slow motion. Selfish, selfish—it flashes in red highlights.

"What are you doing in there? You know I have to dry my hair." She can picture him bending down to pull on his black socks and remembers the dream she has just had while napping—a dream in which her hands and then her arms up to her elbows were coated with soot. She kept trying to get to the sink to wash it off. She was worried in the dream that it wouldn't wash off, but then it had. Everything else in the dream was going wrong. There were dirty dishes in the sink, the walls needed painting, and the party would begin soon.

A trouble-in-mind kind of dream, she calls it, as she peers closely at the shape of her head, which is changing with the haircut.

Before they'd met, he'd seen a picture of her in a book of poetry she'd written. He'd fallen for her, he told her later, because of her words and the wistful, Victorian look on her face. Hollow cheeks and eyes. And why had she cut her hair? After his comment she'd gone in and examined her boy-short cropped look—what women were doing then. It was ten years later. What did he expect? She'd been wearing a nightgown in the picture. She had a hangover. A lover had snapped it as a joke. For years men had declared love for that Victorian suffering. She'd been getting ready to brush her teeth, she protested. Those dark circles? Eye makeup that smeared. Drinking can do that for you. He'd just ignored her, laughing in disbelief and closing his eyes again to find her.

She'd tried to grow it out for the wedding. What she achieved was an aging wood nymph. Her hair had suddenly turned curly again. After all those years, a betrayal like this. She knew then she was lost. It didn't drop limp and tragic looking. It wound in knots and wood-shaving big loops around her face. It grew out, not down. She dyed it red and ordered a wreath of flowers, a crown of charm, to distract him. He forgave her. He wasn't a bad person. He just couldn't understand how her hair happened this way.

"I'm writing fiction," she told him.

"Besides," he calls to her, "it's a matter of being responsible, that's all." She can feel him getting closer and hurries her scissors on the path around the top of her head. A little off each side and the back, where she never looks because when she does, she sees how the hair falls away from the cowlicks exposing the nude scalp. She'll just cut a row along the back there, and maybe it will bend to hide the holes.

When her hair was long, it split like a fork in the road over those places. The curls nestled like forest undergrowth with an occasional peek of ground beneath. Or a head of snakes. The scissors glitter with possibility for a moment.

"Come on, I'm not trying to be hard on you." His voice arrives before he does.

She gives a couple of blind clips to the front, leaving half the curly bangs for a jaunty effect, and gathers two more fistfuls of hair from the sink, as he fills the doorway.

"Can I get in here now?" He looks handsome in his suit. With his boyish good looks he always looks like a kid dressed up for church.

"Do you like my hair?" she asks, as she always does. He nods and unhooks the hair dryer from the back of the door without looking at her. "No really, do you like it? I gave myself a haircut."

He looks at the telltale worms of hair in the sink. "I wondered what this was." Then he plugs in the dryer and turns on its noise.

She waits, standing in his way in front of the mirror while she tries to get the top, an inch long now, to behave like hair, not a crew cut.

"It makes your face rounder, you know," he says.

She smiles and nods. "I know." She's left the curly length in back and along the sides. It is an altogether satisfactory haircut. He shrugs.

The Magician's Assistant

AFTER THE FIRST WEEK he shoved his card in her hand. He had crossed out Lois and printed Marla above it in black ink. She wished he'd used ballpoint so it wouldn't run when they did the milk-in-the-pocket trick.

Later people would ask her if they were married, wonder if they were lovers. Marla would only look puzzled when the subject came up. Was that a trick she would be learning?

Benefits and birthday parties were their mainstay. She told him she wouldn't dress in any goofy costumes, though. Nothing with sequins or sweetheart necklines. He bought her a tuxedo like his, only the pant legs were cut off at mid-thigh. The first time she wore it, she felt his eyes travel up her legs like a road to the tunnel of love.

Her friends wanted to know two things: Did he saw her in half? Did he make her disappear?

She watched him handle the rabbits and pigeons matter-of-factly, but when his hand touched her bare skin, it shook for minutes afterward, as if he had held the heart of an elephant.

The main problem was television conjurers who made expensive cars and camels disappear. No one cared about the flick of the wrist, the scarves that came magically to bloom in the palm of the hand.

When she finally asked him where Lois had gone, he stared at her. His face clouded with pain, and his fingers worked the magic on her.

You Belong to Me

THERE IS NOTHING like the act of watching yourself doing something, he decides as he ducks another armful of clothes from above. It isn't even a question of the neighbors seeing him dressed in his wife's flannel nightgown in the backyard at midnight. Above him the sky rains water and his clothes from the bedroom window.

When something whizzes past his head and lands *thunk* in the dead grass behind him, he ducks instinctively, then looks. In the army they told you, "Never look, for Christ's sake," but he does anyway. His shaving stuff. The electric razor plows a little hole for itself like an undetonated bomb. His hand catches for a moment, then finishes reaching for its chrome brightness, and drops it into a pile beside him.

What puzzles him isn't the bombardment of clothes. He probably deserves that. When he said there wasn't room for his stuff, his life, because she took up all the room, she replied, "Fine, move out back. There's all the space in the world." He'd barely had time to duck and grab the first piece of clothing he could find on the floor beside the bed. Of course, he'd hoped for his pants, not her nightgown. Now he knows he looks like the wolf in "Little Red Riding Hood" dressed up as Granny.

He has to be fair, though. That wasn't all he said. They'd had a good enough time in bed. Sure, that's fine now. He doesn't make any of his usual earlier mistakes—telling her that she should hurry or that he's tired when he's finished. He's grown up there—not enough to brag to anyone, but she can't complain about that.

His attention is caught sharply by the record album slicing the air in front of his nose like a Frisbee. Shoot. He looks up and watches albums pour out of the window like paratroopers, then glide gracefully down to stumble and fall on the ground below. He starts to run around grabbing them up in his arms like a man chasing his hat on a windy day, but he stops. The rain is changing to snow, and globs of it begin to clump on the clothes and welt the cardboard record covers. "Goodbye, Willie Nelson," he mouths. "Goodbye, Bruce Springsteen."

"Honey," he calls. "Jo?" Above him her wild face appears, then is gone like the pulse of a neon sign. He waits below, hopeful for the next flash.

What he receives is the pottery pitcher, the first thing they bought together, which explodes at his feet. Bending down to examine it, he realizes that this is the first thing he can feel really sorry about. As he picks up the shards of blue glazed clay, he misses the bulkier things dropping onto the bushes: the framed reproductions of paintings they both liked, the plaster cast of a woman's torso, the pillows off the bed.

It was their courtship, and clumsy as he was at it, he had been sincere. Leaving the safety of his first wife for the breathlessness of this new woman had scared him. Sometimes he felt trapped in a forest fire that was whipping the waves of flame back around him, sucking the air into itself. He had to struggle just to walk upright in the house some days. How did he get here? he'd ask himself.

"I'll huff, and I'll puff, and I'll blow the house down,"

she'd tease him when he went quiet before going home to his wife those first months.

Tonight he feels an unraveling, almost the same as the unwrapping he'd experienced with her that had spun him like some mummy far out of his marriage into her life, un-winding, unwinding, the bandage wrappings held by her effortlessly as he spun like a top between the poles of the two houses, his wife's and hers. Finally, when he was bare again, he settled in with her, coming to her unexpectedly in the middle of the week, carrying a small gym bag with his toiletries and a change of underwear. Just when she'd given up, just when she was going out of town with friends, he arrived on her doorstep like a Girl Scout selling cookies.

Now the shards of pitcher glint and cut at something deeper: the invisible, binding, filament line that holds him perfectly and cruelly in his place. He wonders if he'll have to find someone else now.

No. The broken pitcher is a message he tries to read. What is it saying? What is she saying? He feels like a man stranded on the moon, space-wrecked. He shakes pieces of pottery in his hands like old bones, small rocks of soothsay-ing. What? What?

He doesn't know how long he sits there with the shards at his feet like archaeological remains. He stops wondering what to do. He stops worrying about the snow, which begins to crust him over, sticking coldly to her nightgown and his feet and hands sticking out of the cloth. He doesn't know his eyes are closed until her hand, brushing his face and hair, tells him.

"Are you okay?" she asks, as she tucks his overcoat around his shoulders.

"I guess you're not that hard to live with," he says, but all he can hear is the wind rising in the elm tree above them.

"Come on." She pulls at his arm, trying to get him up. He watches her do it. Maybe she's the tar baby he's stuck to.

Please don't throw me in the brier patch, he thinks. Then he gets confused. What happens to the tar baby? Is the rabbit stuck with a friend for life?

"Don't," he says, meaning the brier patch.

"It's okay. I made some truth serum. We'll go in, get dry."

He is walking then, watching himself: a snowman moving on thick chunks of legs back into the house. He doesn't think about his things in the backyard, only the hot rum waiting in cups with a chunk of butter slicking the surface to make it go down more easily. "Truth serum"— they've named it for the way it makes their talks glide.

Toward morning they will return to the bedroom, where it started. And he will tell her of his relief now that all his things are gone. He can get a clean start, and he'll feel that something important is true here. When she offers to let him throw her stuff out the window to make it even, he smiles and holds her close, rubbing her skull with the gentle intentness of Aladdin polishing his lamp.